PEN FRIEND FROM ANOTHER PLANET

Andersen Young Readers' Library

PEN FRIEND FROM ANOTHER PLANET

PHILIP CURTIS

Illustrated by Tony Ross

Andersen Press · London

For Camilla Curtis

Text © 1990 by Philip Curtis
Illustrations © 1990 by Tony Ross

First published in Great Britain in 1990 by
Andersen Press Limited
20 Vauxhall Bridge Road, London SW1V 2SA

This edition first published in 2000

British Library Cataloguing in Publication Data available

ISBN 0 86264 970 6

Typesetting by Print Origination (NW) Limited, Formby, Liverpool L37 8EG
Printed and bound in Great Britain by Guernsey Press Company Limited,
Guernsey, Channel Islands

Contents

1

Floating in the Wind

The new Class 4C sat quietly, all eyes on their new teacher as she called the register for the first time.

'Christopher Collings!' she called out.

'Yes, Miss!' Chris, a tall, thin boy with unruly dark hair, sat up very straight as the teacher picked him out with her eyes. He was sitting near the back of the classroom, and he thought he knew what was going on in the teacher's mind. It wouldn't be long before she moved him to a place nearer her own desk. Now, though, she passed on to the next name.

The new class was called 6C because they were in the top year of Fairfield Junior School, and their teacher's name was Miss Camperdown - called 'Campers' for short. They all knew Miss Camperdown well, for in their earlier years she had taught them from time to time. She was a tall lady with fair, wavy hair, who liked playing netball with the girls because she could almost hand the ball through the ring to score a goal without having to throw it, when she stood on tiptoe.

Most of the class were not too sure what to

expect from her, because at times she could be very dreamy and have her mind on something far away from school work, and at others she could be terribly strict as if to make up for it. Girls who wanted to be in the netball team were happiest to be in her class, and boys who tended to be untidy, like Chris, were looking forward to the coming year much more warily.

But Miss Camperdown seemed to have enjoyed her summer holiday very much, and said she was looking forward to the coming school year with Class 6C.

'I have something rather interesting to tell you, Class 6C,' she said. 'But it will have to wait until the end of the afternoon, because we have all our books to arrange - and our class positions. For a start, Chris Collings and Gordon Welsh, come out to the front. I want you to sit in this group here - with Mary Francom, Jill Murray and the other three children already sitting here.'

The morning until playtime was spent in shuffling the children into positions which she fancied, and in making out a timetable and writing names on books.

'She didn't take long to move us,' said Chris at playtime to his friend Gordon.

'It had to be,' said Gordon, 'but she seems all right so far.'

'I wonder what she has to tell us,' said Mary

Francom, a small, dark-haired girl who looked like being one of the favourites of Miss Camperdown, because she was the best netball player in the class.

'Nothing exciting, really, I expect,' said Gordon. 'Perhaps that we'll be the first to take a Class Assembly.'

'Perhaps she's going to get married,' suggested Jill, who took great pleasure in planning the lives of teachers.

'I wouldn't marry her!' declared Gordon. 'She'd always be telling you what to do.'

The idea of the plump, red-cheeked Gordon marrying Miss Camperdown made both the girls giggle - and ended discussion of the subject.

As the day wore on, Chris and Gordon began to think that being in Miss Camperdown's class wouldn't be so bad after all. There were two top year classes at Fairfield School, and Chris and Gordon had both hoped that they might be in Mr Wilton's class. Mr Wilton took the football team, and was very keen to take his class out to a nearby pond for science lessons, which were very popular. But he took the older children of the year group, and Chris missed out by a couple of weeks and Gordon by three months.

Mr Wilton had a name for playing the guitar, whereas Miss Camperdown was known to be, at

9

times, a nagger. On this first day, though, the boys had no reason to complain. She moved about the classroom happily enough, and assured the class that all would be well as long as they behaved themselves. By mid afternoon she entered into a dreamy stage, now and then staring out of the window and smiling to herself. With half an hour left she sat down happily at her desk and asked the children to describe any especially interesting holiday happenings they could remember.

Even the funniest holiday stories can become boring after a while, and Chris and Gordon became a little restless. In the end Gordon put up his hand.

'Well, Gordon, and where did you go this summer?'

'Nowhere, Miss. Please, Miss, where did you go?'

The class waited with interest to see whether Miss Camperdown would reply to this. To their surprise she didn't tell Gordon off, nor did she call upon him to describe something which had happened to him while at home.

'As a matter of fact, Gordon, I spent most of the holiday in France,' she said, speaking as if the very name of France gave her pleasure. 'Have any of you been to France?' she asked, and when several hands were raised she looked

with approval at their owners.

'It's a beautiful country,' she said dreamily - and then sat up straight with a jerk. 'Has anyone anything else to tell me?' There was no movement, for by now all the keen talkers had talked.

'Please, Miss,' said Chris, 'you said you had something interesting to tell us this afternoon, and it's almost time for the bell - '

'Yes, Chris, you are quite right, and talking of France brings me to that very point. I met a teacher over there, and he wants some pen friends for his children. They will write in English to you at first, because they have already started learning English. We hope that later on you will be able to learn some French. I may even teach you a little myself. First of all I must find out how many of you would like to have pen friends. The French children live in a pretty little town near the Atlantic Ocean. Who knows, some of you might make friends and go and visit them there, especially now the Channel Tunnel is open. Now let me take the names of those who would be keen to reply to their letters.'

Everyone in the class was keen - and Miss Camperdown noted down the numbers of boys and girls. 'And now you must jot down on paper what your hobbies are,' she declared. 'Chris and Mary, give out these sheets of paper. Write your names and birthday dates on them, and then put down all the things you like to do.'

There was silence for a while. Chris wrote on his paper: 'Sports - Football and Swimming. Hobbies - collecting stamps, watching T.V. and reading (mostly Space books). I have one sister (eight years old) and a BMX bike. I live in a house with four bedrooms and a big garden, and my dad has a car.'

That, he thought, should be enough to attract

the interest of any French boy. Miss Camperdown took the pieces of paper in order to send them off with a letter of her own to the French teacher.

Days went by, and the days turned into weeks, and Miss Camperdown had to tell the children every now and then to be patient.

'This kind of arrangement takes time,' she said. 'It shouldn't be many more days now.'

By the time the letters from France did come - inside a large envelope addressed to Miss Camperdown - boys like Chris and Gordon had forgotten all about them. Miss Camperdown read the letter addressed to herself with great interest.

'Now, children,' she said. 'I'll call out your names and give you your first letters. After this, you'll have to post your own letters yourselves, and the replies will come to your homes direct.'

She began to call out names, and the children collected their letters one by one. Gordon and Chris watched and listened as their friends brought them back and began to read them, some of them laughing over their pen friends' English.

'Listen to this,' giggled Mary. 'My friend is called Cecile, and she wants to come to England to go up to the top of Nelson's Column in the Piccadilly.'

'Don't laugh at their mistakes!' said Miss Camperdown sternly. 'I wonder how much you know of France, and how many words of French you can speak. Gordon Welsh,' she added, 'here's your letter - and that's the last one.'

Gordon hurried from his seat and collected the letter, and Chris put up his hand.

'Please, Miss, I haven't had a letter!'

Miss Camperdown looked at him in surprise and some doubt, but saw that he was speaking the truth.

'That's funny, Chris,' she said, and looked around on her desk, picked up the big envelope and tore it wide open, and then inspected the floor around her.

'Are you sure you haven't had one, Chris? There aren't any more in here.'

'Of course I haven't, Miss!' replied Chris. 'You didn't call out my name.'

'Odd,' said Miss Camperdown. 'I'm sure I sent off all your sheets to France. I'll mention it to Monsieur Legrand when I write next. I'm sorry, Chris.'

Chris hadn't really been much bothered about having a French pen friend until now, when he saw all the rest comparing their letters.

'Hard luck, Chris,' said Gordon, meaning well. 'Have a look at mine.'

Chris tossed the letter back angrily.

'I don't want yours!' he grumbled. 'I want one

14

of my own.'

'Now, Chris,' said Miss Camperdown, 'don't be bad tempered. It's not Gordon's fault that you haven't had a letter.'

To make matters worse for him, she started reading her own letter again, and finding much pleasure in it, while the children all read theirs. Chris was glad when they had to put their letters away and go back to ordinary work. That night he lay in bed and couldn't sleep because he hadn't received a letter - which surprised him, for he still couldn't quite believe that a letter could mean so much to him.

In the end he resorted to a habit which he had taken to when a day had not been too happy. He tried to imagine himself out of his own body and floating in space, drifting ever further away from the world into endless emptiness. When he opened his eyes again, the wallpaper and the ceiling seemed strange and distant, as though he were seeing it properly for the first time. After a while his attempts to float into space led to drowsiness and sleep.

When he awoke the next morning he remembered the disappointment of the letter, and he was in silent and thoughtful mood as he sat down to breakfast.

'Whatever is the matter, Chris?' his mother asked. 'Something gone wrong at school?'

'No, nothing, Mum.'

'Well, cheer up, then.'

He tried to do so, and by the time he reached the school playground had almost succeeded. He found that his friends had forgotten about their letters - and maybe when it came to sitting down and writing a reply they had found the idea of a pen friend not quite as exciting as it had been when they received them. All might then have been well for the rest of the day, had not Miss Camperdown made a big mistake.

When the class had settled down to work, she called Chris out to her desk.

'About your pen friend, Chris,' she began. 'I was on the phone to Monsieur Legrand last night, and I told him you hadn't received a letter.'

'Yes, Miss?'

'And it seems that the boy who was to write to you has suddenly moved from the district. There's nobody else of your age to take his place. Monsieur Legrand said that if necessary he could contact another school, but I think it would not be easy. It is better for the children to be able to talk with their teacher about the letters. I told him I didn't think you'd mind, Chris. After all, I don't suppose you are very keen on writing letters.'

'I suppose I'm not, Miss.'

'Good, then. I didn't want you to be upset about it. All right, Chris - you may sit down now.'

Miss Camperdown clearly believed that Chris wasn't upset - and that made matters worse for him. The truth was, perhaps, that she didn't want to upset Monsieur Legrand, and was thinking so much about his phone call that she wasn't quite her usual self that morning.

In any case, she was hopelessly, unforgivably wrong, and Chris gave her a bad time of it for the rest of the day. He sulked, he fidgeted, he annoyed other children and he even had a fight in the playground with Gordon for no real reason at all. When it was over, he said he was sorry to Gordon, because he knew he had picked the quarrel himself.

'What's the matter, Chris?' asked Gordon. 'Is something wrong?'

'No, nothing!' replied Chris, who couldn't bear to talk about the letters.

When school was at last over, he invited Gordon to come with him to Fairfield Park and look for conkers - the time of year was just right for them.

'Sorry, Chris,' said Gordon, making things worse without realising it. 'I want to go home and write my letter to my pen friend, Pierre.'

'Oh, go home, then!' Angrily Chris kicked a

stone into the road, where it clanged against the wheel of a passing car. It looked as if the driver of the car might slow down and stop - so Chris and Gordon ran off in different directions. Chris had not intended to go to the park on his own, but he was running in that direction, and so in his anger he kept going.

Several people looked at the tall, dark-haired, pale boy who was running so fast and so earnestly, as if he had somewhere very special to go. Chris hadn't, of course, and when he reached the park he wondered why he had come. The horse chestnuts were still securely on the branches of the trees, and he didn't fancy annoying the park-keeper by throwing stones up at them. Instead, he made his way along the narrow path up to the Fairfield Rock. This was the only unusual feature of Fairfield Park. The path led in a spiral up a large mound, and on top of it stood a huge rock. Some people said that the rock had been hurled there by the Devil, and suggested that there should be an entrance fee charged to go and see it. Wiser heads, however, realised that the rock was not big enough nor high enough to make it worth anybody paying to see it, as it could be plainly seen from down below. So it remained there free for all. It was mostly used by boys in their games. They loved to attack or defend it, and to throw things down

18

from it at their friends.

Chris reached the top of the path and scrambled up on the rock - an easy task for his long legs. He was all alone on the rock, and he stood there and stared up at the sky and wondered why he had been so unlucky. There were clouds in the sky, and a small break between two of them gave the effect of a tunnel leading to a small circle of blue sky. In his unhappy mood Chris stared through this hole, wishing he could escape to some other world - just as he had done in bed the night before.

As he gazed through the gap in the clouds his mind became locked on it, just as radar equipment might lock itself on an enemy plane. The hole, in a curious way, was coming nearer, and was shaped like a cloudy funnel, the widest end of it being nearest to Chris, and the far end now opening on a mere pinprick of blue sky. As the funnel came nearer, Chris heard a whirring sound, and saw that the cloudy sides of the funnel were constantly moving around, as if currents of air were controlling them and keeping them from blocking the funnel.

As the funnel came down Chris dimly realised that if it came on further he would be in the middle of the hole, with clouds surging all around him; but like a scared rabbit, he was unable to stir from the spot, powerless to escape

19

from whatever might be coming his way.

Suddenly clouds were all around him, and in a moment of panic he imagined himself being sucked into the hole. Then all became still, except for a tiny object floating down the funnel. It fluttered from side to side as it came down, moving like a butterfly. Chris watched it as if hypnotised as it descended until it was only head high. He could have stretched out and grasped it, but it looked so delicate and flimsy that he was afraid it might crumble to pieces in his hand. He allowed it to flutter gently on downwards, and it finally came to rest at his feet. As it did so, the clouds around the funnel began to close in, until there was no hole to be seen at all; then like mist in the sun, the clouds rose up and dispersed. In a few seconds the sky was as it had been before, cloudy with one or two clear patches here and there.

Chris could have believed that the funnel had never existed, were it not for the piece of white material lying at his feet. Looking around him to see that he was still alone, he bent down and carefully put a finger underneath it, still afraid that it would fall to pieces like the ash from a burnt piece of paper. The material remained firm, though, and he risked trying to pick it up, scooping the fingers of both hands beneath it. To his surprise it came up in one piece, and ap-

peared to be in no danger of breaking. It was rectangular in shape, and though it looked like a whitish-grey piece of paper, it could be bent and twisted as easily as a piece of cloth.

Chris held it up to the light to examine it closely. There were no marks on it other than lots of tiny dots, no bigger than pinpricks, which stood out on the material in the same way as Braille writing for the blind does.

Though there didn't seem much point in keeping it, the way it had appeared was mysterious, and for that reason he put it in his pocket and took it home. There he went to his bedroom to inspect his find more closely before throwing it away. He rummaged in a drawer and brought out a magnifying glass. Putting the material on a window ledge, he studied it carefully through the lens. The result was slightly disappointing. There was nothing to be seen except the pinprick sized marks which covered most of one side of the material, which for want of a better name Chris thought of as paper.

He was still curious about it, but decided not to mention it to his parents, who might remove all the mystery from it by explaining what it was. He couldn't face another disappointment that day. For the same reason he didn't show it to his sister Laura, for she would only laugh at him. So the paper stayed in his trouser pocket that evening and all night long, and he took it with him to school in the morning.

He waited until playtime before speaking to Gordon about it.

'I've something to show you, Gordon,' he said. 'I can't make out exactly what it is.'

'Where did you get it?' asked the practical Gordon, when given a quick look at the paper.

'I'll tell you that later,' said Chris, who had already decided that if Gordon found nothing of interest in the paper, he wouldn't risk telling him the strange story of the funnel. 'Come with me and we'll look at it behind the sports store,' he added. He didn't want numbers of curious on-lookers to be present while Gordon gave his verdict.

On their way to the back of the store they passed Mary Francom, who was managing to skip and talk with her friend Jill at the same time.

'Did you see that sort of tornado over the fields yesterday?' Mary was asking. 'I thought it was coming down over my house, but it stayed somewhere near the park.'

Mary lived near the park. Jill shook her head and skipped energetically.

'It doesn't seem to have done any damage,' admitted Mary, and then saved her breath for the skipping.

'I saw that tornado thing,' said Gordon.

'So did I,' remarked Chris, trying to appear very casual about it.

Behind the store he took out the piece of paper and passed it to Gordon, who had clearly expected to be shown something more exciting. To please his friend he held it up to the light and then passed his fingers over it.

'Funny stuff they make these days,' he said. 'It seems to be covered with dots - '

'That's right,' said Chris.

'Dots and dashes,' went on Gordon, suddenly showing much more interest. He turned the paper round another way and inspected it much more closely and seriously. 'Yes,' he added, 'some of these marks are longer than others. I think you could say they are dashes. You know what that means.'

'What does it mean?' asked Chris.

'It means that there could be a message written on it in Morse Code,' declared Gordon. 'Secret messages can be sent that way - they used it in the last war, and my grandad used to use it.'

'What does it say?' asked Chris, looking troubled.

'I can't remember all the letters,' admitted Gordon. 'These three dots could stand for an "S" - as in S.O.S., you know. But I can sort it out for you, if you want me to. I've been reading a book about it at home, and it has all the letters listed. Come round to my house after school, and we'll try and decode it.'

The rest of the day passed normally, and now and then Chris forgot all about the paper tucked away in his pocket. He went home with Gordon, and on the way called in on his mother to tell her he was going to Gordon's house, which was not far away.

Gordon quickly produced his encyclopedia and found the piece on the Morse Code.

'You can see the little gaps between the letters,' said Gordon, studying the paper. 'You call out the dots and dashes, and I'll look up the letters and write them down.'

'It's going to be pretty boring,' said Chris, looking at the hundreds of dots and dashes on the paper.

'If it's too boring, or doesn't make sense, we can always stop,' declared Gordon. 'Give me the first letter - oh, all right, I can see it, "D". Now go on.'

'Dot,' said Chris.

'E,' said Gordon, and wrote it down.

'Dot-dash is next.'

'A,' reported Gordon.

'Dot-dash-dot.'

'R,' declared Gordon. 'Why, that makes the

word "Dear".'

'Go on, Gordon,' urged Chris. 'Dash-dot-dash-dot is next.'

'C,' said Gordon.

'Four dots,' Chris told him.

'That's H,' said Gordon.

'Dot-dash-dot again,' went on Chris, growing more and more excited.

'R again,' reported Gordon, and the same thought struck him as had been exciting Chris for the last couple of letters. 'Surely it's not a letter to you, Chris?'

'Dot-dot,' said Chris, and then: 'Dot-dot-dot.'

'That's it!' cried Gordon. ' "Dear Chris." '

He turned almost angrily to Chris.

'You're having me on, aren't you?' he demanded.

'No, no, honestly I'm not. I swear it!' replied Chris, and he looked so pale and excited that Gordon had to believe him.

'Let's get on with it, then,' he said, and gradually they worked through all the dots and dashes, and finished up with a letter to Chris which took up most of a full sheet of notepaper.

'Where did you get this?' asked Gordon, and this time Chris was only too pleased to talk about it.

'The paper floated down to me in the park yesterday. I was standing on the rock, and the kind of whirlwind Mary was talking about came down, and this piece of - of stuff landed at my feet. It was just like that, honest it was, Gordon!'

'If that's true, then you have a pen friend after all, Chris,' said Gordon. 'A pen friend from space!'

They sat and read the letter through once more, concentrating more than they had ever done over any piece of writing.

2

Secret Post Office

Still hardly able to believe what he saw, Chris read the letter out loud.

' "Dear Chris, It has become known to me that you have been trying to contact another planet because you feel alone and unwanted on your own. This dream of yours would be an impossible one, but for a most strange chance. The nearest planet to yours with intelligent life on it is so far away from you that your scientists will not be able to discover it for hundreds of years yet, and even then the thought of being in touch with it would be absurd. It so happens, though, that we, the masters of time and the winds, are making a tour of your universe, and are studying the state of life on the planets round your sun. We see much misery and unhappiness on your earth, and have received thought messages from many people. We cannot help them - but your message came to me, the youngest member of our expedition, and I begged to be allowed to write to you. My father at last gave his permission, and so we arranged for you to go to the highest place near to you in order to receive this letter. Chris, you now have a pen friend from the spacecraft *Passim*, which will be in touch with your world for some time to come. I would like to know more about your life, and will tell you about mine and try to answer your questions. All my father asks is that our letters must be kept between ourselves and friends of our own age. We have mastered the messages we have heard sent in the same language in different parts of the world, and will you please use the same way of writing when you reply. You can write on the same piece of paper. First put it in water, and all the marks will vanish. You may reply on what paper you wish, but if you do not do so on this, please make sure that it is destroyed by putting it in water. When you wish to send your reply, go again to the place where you received this letter, put yours on the ground at your feet, and think hard of me and of the spacecraft *Passim*. I am looking forward to hearing from you. My name is hard to put into your language, so it is easier if you call me Peter. Write to me soon.

Peter. A.R." '

'What's the A.R. for?' asked Chris

'That's the way they end messages in Morse,' said Gordon, after studying the book. He looked closely at his friend again. 'Promise me, Chris, that you haven't made all this up!' he said.

'How could I?' replied Chris angrily. 'I don't even know about Morse Code - you must realise that!'

'Are you going to write back?' asked Gordon.

'Of course I am. But you'll have to help me, Gordon, and it's going to take quite a while to put the letter into Morse Code.'

'Are you going to show this to anyone else?'

'Not this one,' said Chris, after thinking for a while. 'Let's put it in water, Gordon, and see what happens to it.'

'Better try it upstairs in the bathroom,' said Gordon, 'in case my mum comes in.'

He led the way upstairs, and after a final, curious look at it, they placed the letter in a basinful of water. At first it rested on the surface, and Chris pressed it down with his hand so that it was completely immersed.

'Is it going?' asked Gordon, peering into the basin.

'Don't know - I'll hold it under a little longer. That's odd - the water's becoming warmer. Try it yourself, Gordon.'

Gordon put his finger in the water, and agreed with Chris.

'And the water came cold out of the tap,' he added.

'The paper must be making some sort of energy,' decided Chris, whose favourite subject

in school was science. Miss Camperdown only gave them small rations of science at school, because usually it was too messy for her, so Chris sometimes did experiments at home.

'It's not becoming any hotter,' he said after they had waited for a minute or two. 'I'm going to take the paper out.'

He held the paper over the basin and let the water drip off it. Then he held it up to the window.

'It's true!' he said. 'All the dots and dashes have gone. It's turned a little bit greyer, but it's perfectly smooth. See for yourself.'

'You're right,' agreed Gordon, looking at his friend with a mixture of bewilderment and admiration. 'When are we going to write back?'

'I shall start tomorrow,' said Chris, 'but it's going to be a long job. Will you bring your book to school tomorrow, and we can start in the dinner hour. We'll have to make sure we're on our own - I don't want anybody else to know about it.'

'I won't say anything, I promise,' declared Gordon.

As they went downstairs, Gordon's mother appeared, and Chris swiftly slipped the letter into his pocket.

'What have you two been up to?' she asked.

'Nothing,' replied Gordon. 'We were playing football in the garden, and we went upstairs to wash our hands.'

The excuse was accepted, and Chris went home with the letter safely in his pocket, realising now that to keep his new pen friend a secret from the rest of the world might place him in some awkward situations. Since nothing more exciting might ever happen to him in his whole life, he felt it would be right to put people off with excuses not altogether true if necessary. He was pleased, though, that he could talk to one friend about it, otherwise the secret might have become too breath-taking for him to bear alone.

The letter stayed under his pillow that night, for safety's sake, and the task of replying to it was on his mind as he lay sleepless for a long time above it.

The next day the planning of the reply was begun. Chris and Gordon found a sloping corner of the school field where they could be away from the after dinner games of football and the various playground activities. Now and again girls picking the last daisies of the year came near them, but they were ready for this. At any sign of danger Chris pocketed the letter and they went on studying the book, pretending to be learning about the Morse Code.

They learned how quickly time passes when you are really concentrating, for they had only managed the opening sentences when a teacher appeared and rang a handbell to warn them that afternoon school was about to begin. They continued work after school at Chris's house, where his little sister became a nuisance.

'What are you doing?' she demanded when she had broken into the room for the third time.

'We're busy with some homework,' replied Chris with a lofty air. 'Please go away and play somewhere else.'

She grumbled, but obeyed, and they were able to work on until Chris's mother told them a meal would be ready soon, and Gordon realised that he had better go home before questions were asked there. They stopped for the day, with dots and dashes flickering in front of their eyes. The following day they carried on as they had done at dinner time the day before, and now it was Mary Francom who became a nuisance. Pretending to look for daisies, she came nearer and nearer to them in zigzags, and then pounced.

'What's going on?' she demanded. 'I've never seen you two so quiet before. You haven't moved from here for half an hour.'

Chris whisked the piece of paper they were working on into his pocket, a difficult operation because Mary had one hand resting heavily on his shoulder and the other on Gordon's.

'Mind your own business,' said Gordon, and this brought the response they could have expected.

'Why should I? And what's that you've just put in your pocket, Chris?'

She made a grab for Chris's pocket, and only by rolling over on one side and lying on it did he prevent her from pulling out the paper.

'We're only learning the Morse Code,' explained Gordon. 'Just because you're jealous, you don't need to spend your time trying to upset people who do have something to do!'

This, of course, made Mary even madder, but in the scrimmage that followed she forgot all about the paper - at least for some days. Gordon and Chris couldn't settle to work again, and so the letter remained unfinished for yet another day.

It was two days later when the reply was finished, and Chris and Gordon made plans to go to the park after lessons.

'May I come with you to see if anything happens?' asked Gordon. Chris couldn't refuse him after all the work he'd done, yet felt that he should be alone when the posting of the letter took place - if it did. By now both he and Gordon were beginning to have doubts, though neither wanted to tell the other of this.

'You can come to the foot of the rock,' said Chris after some thought, 'but I ought to be alone with the letter on the rock. With two of us there, maybe nothing would happen.'

Gordon looked at him slightly suspiciously, but agreed. The two of them found the afternoon lessons with Miss Camperdown extremely long and boring, and both of them kept on looking at their watches. Miss Camperdown, who was having one of her irritable times, perhaps because she hadn't heard from Monsieur Legrand lately, caught them at it.

'All you two boys have done this afternoon is to check what the time is,' she complained. 'Have you something so very important to do after school that you can't give your minds to your work?'

'No, Miss,' said Chris, turning red in the face and so arousing the suspicions of Mary, who was sitting opposite him.

'Well, then, don't look at those watches any more, or I shall take them from you until after school - and keep you in after school as well.'

The afternoon dragged on, and they tried to interest themselves in the topic which they were working on, which by chance was the Post Office. At last the bell rang, and they put their books away and sat up straight like animals begging for food. It must have been out of spite that Miss Camperdown kept their group back until last, but in the end she had to let them go.

'You were trying too hard to look good,' said Mary as they went along the corridor. 'Are you going to a party?'

'No,' replied Gordon.

'Then what's the hurry?'

'There's no hurry,' said Chris. 'We were just bored.'

Mary believed this for a while, until she saw them dash off down the road in the direction of the park. She thought of following them, but decided she had better things to do, such as watching her favourite television programme.

So Chris and Gordon were on their own, well ahead of any others possibly heading in the direction of the park. To Chris's relief he found the path up the mound around the rock deserted.

'You stay here, Gordon,' he said, 'and don't try and come up until I call you. Remember, I have to do some thinking before anything will happen, so give me a little time.'

'Oh, all right.' Gordon was none too pleased to be left out at the last minute, but he knew he had agreed to it, so stayed down below while Chris climbed the path to the rock.

When he reached the top of the rock Chris waved down to Gordon, and then turned away and put the letter down at his feet. Earnestly he made himself think only of his new pen friend Peter and of the spacecraft *Passim*. He stared up into the sky, trying to tear himself away from the world as he had done before when he lay in bed, but right at the back of his mind there remained a tiny fear that he might be let down again, and nothing would happen. Rather than go down to Gordon and admit failure, he decided he would destroy the letter and pretend it had all been a joke. The thought of this was so depressing that he gazed up at the sky again, begging for some-

37

thing to happen. If only a high wind would come and blow the wretched letter away!

Even as he thought, a breeze floated around the rock and fanned Chris's face, and at the same time clouds formed in the sky above him. Dimly he was aware of a funnel of air above him.

At his feet, the letter became alive, hopping a little to one side and then back again. The whirring sound he had heard before on the rock began again, and then the letter rose in the air, swaying gently from side to side, until it was away above his head and in the centre of the funnel. Then, like a piece of fluff disappearing into a vacuum cleaner, the paper was sucked upwards and out of sight, leaving Chris staring into the clouds. Gradually the wind died down. He looked at his feet, to make sure the letter had really gone, and then ran down the spiral path to rejoin Gordon, who was waiting patiently at the foot of the path.

'It's gone!' cried Chris.

'I know,' said Gordon, 'I could see it floating upwards. It's all true, Chris - but what do we do now?'

'We can only wait until we have a reply,' said Chris.

'Do we have to come to the park every day to see if anything's happened?' asked Gordon. Chris

shook his head.

'I have a feeling that I shall know when to go there,' he said. 'I can't say how - we'll just have to wait and see.'

They walked most of the way home in silence, each busy with his own thoughts. Turning a corner, they came face to face with Mary, who was on her way home from a friend's house. Their serious expressions once more aroused her suspicions.

'Hullo, you two - where have you come from? A secret mission, perhaps? You must be planning something - you've been acting strangely all day.'

'Sorry to disappoint you,' said Chris, 'but we've just been to the park to look for conkers, and it seems to be too early for them.'

'Shame!' called out Mary as she walked away.

When Chris thought about what they had really been doing, he wondered whether he would ever again be content to interest himself in such ordinary activities as collecting conkers.

3

Masters of the Winds

In the days that followed Chris often thought about his letter and wondered what kind of reply it might bring. He had described himself in it, told his pen friend what his main interests were, and asked in return for a short description of Peter and of his planet.

A week passed, and although he paid one or two visits to the rock he found nothing there.

'Maybe that's the end of it,' suggested Gordon. 'Perhaps your pen friend doesn't think it worth replying - or his spacecraft has moved on somewhere else.'

Gordon said this with a grin playing around his lips, and Chris was irritated as he realised that his friend was already beginning to doubt once more whether the first letter really had come from space. Unfortunately at the same time Miss Camperdown became irritated too, because her own pen friend, Monsieur Legrand, had not replied directly to her own last letter.

'Chris Collings!' she would call out sharply from time to time. 'Don't sit there dreaming! Get on with your work!'

Chris would make an effort to concentrate, but

it was usually not long before she was at him again. He was always pleased to go home in the afternoon, but even there he could not settle to do the modelling he was so keen on, nor could he settle to watch television. One night he went up early to his bedroom and stared out into the darkness. He could hear the wind moaning in the distance. Could his letter be on the way? The planet Venus was shining brightly and steadily in the sky - perhaps his pen friend had moved on to inspect it.

Suddenly, not far from Venus, he saw a bright light moving from side to side. Each time it swayed, the light became a little brighter, as though it were coming nearer. The light was circular in shape, and it was moving in exactly the same way as his letter had done. The sound of the wind became louder, and very soon a small hurricane was blowing around the house. The light of the swaying object became so bright that he had to shade his eyes, and he couldn't look directly into it. Curtains were pulled back in houses opposite as other people became aware of the strange light.

Then, as if aware that it was drawing too much attention to itself, the disc turned with its sharp edge to the earth and moved swiftly away like a penny rolling down a hill. Soon there was nothing more to see, and the high winds also died away. Chris went downstairs and said nothing about what he had seen - but the next morning the school playground was buzzing with reports of sightings of the strange light.

'Did you see that UFO in the sky last night?' asked Steve Brownlee. 'My dad took a photo of it, and he's sending it to the local UFO Society.'

If the children were excited, so was the local press, which printed the reports of sightings by several local people, including a policeman, a bus driver and an amateur astronomer, who had watched the light through a telescope.

'The object appeared to be using air currents to assist its movement,' he told the reporter. 'It could have been a spacecraft, but just as I thought I could detect its shape and size, it turned on its side and disappeared in a flash.'

A few days later an article by a professional astronomer appeared, in which he claimed that exciting though the light had been to the various observers, the probable cause was the movement of a shooting star or meteorite, which was something which often happens in autumn.

Chris was not convinced.

'The light was moving from side to side in the same way that my letter did,' he told Gordon. 'I don't think anybody knows what it really was, and they're just trying to explain it as best they can. I believe it could have been the spacecraft

43

Passim.'

Gordon shrugged his shoulders, and nothing more was said about the mysterious light until a day later, when, to the surprise of Chris, Mary Francom began to talk about it during a silent reading lesson. Mary and her friend Jill were sitting in the same group and almost opposite Chris and Gordon, and a moment for conversation came when Miss Camperdown moved to the back of the classroom in order to pin up some pictures on the wall.

'I couldn't sleep last night,' whispered Mary to Jill. 'I was awake at three o'clock, and I thought it was nearly morning because of a strange light in the room. I went to the window, and in the distance was the same light that everyone was talking about a few days back, only this time it was facing my room like a plate, wobbling a bit, and although it was further away than the moon, its rays seemed to be heading straight for me. I was just going to wake my parents up, when it turned to one side and disappeared. I couldn't sleep for quite a while after that, because I thought it might be coming back. I was afraid, Jill, I suppose because it was the middle of the night, and I felt it was shining directly on me.'

'Didn't your parents see it?' asked Jill.

'No - they sleep in the front of the house,' said Mary. 'I told them about it in the morning,

and they'd slept the whole night through. I don't believe it was an asteroid, or a meteorite, or whatever they've been saying.'

'Did it move from side to side?' asked Chris, suddenly joining in the conversation.

'Why - have you seen it too?' asked Mary sharply.

'Not last night,' said Chris, 'but I have seen it.'

'It was already there when I first looked out,' said Mary, 'and when it disappeared I went back to bed because it was cold standing by the window. When did you see it swaying about?'

'Oh, some days back,' said Chris.

'When? In the night? Did it wake you up?'

Mary's dark eyes seemed as though they were trying to penetrate his head. Once she was interested in something, she always persisted until she had found out all she could about it. The fair-haired, rather dreamy Jill, on the other hand, had already returned to her book.

'Well - yes, I saw it a few nights back,' admitted Chris, 'when all the others did. But I also saw something swaying about in the daytime. Was it as if it was being blown backwards and forwards by the wind? You said it was wobbling a bit.'

'I suppose it could have been like that,' agreed Mary. 'Why are you so interested in its wobbling from side to side?'

'It might be important,' said Gordon, wishing to take part in the conversation. 'It might be - '

'Shut up!' said Chris sharply - just as Miss Camperdown was coming back from sticking pins in the wall.

'Chris Collings, this is supposed to be a silent reading lesson, not a conversation class!' she snapped. 'And I don't like the expression "shut up". Go out to the front with your book. You can stand there on your own for a while, just to show you that when I say reading I mean reading. And I don't want to hear another word from any of you others in the group!'

That put an end to further discussion of the strange light, but after school Chris had a word with Gordon on their way home.

'You nearly gave the game away to Mary,' he grumbled. 'If I hadn't stopped you, would you have told her that it was the letter which I saw swaying from side to side?'

'I don't know,' replied Gordon, looking puzzled. 'Something came over me and made me speak. I was so surprised by what Mary said.'

'Be a bit more careful in future!' Chris warned him. 'I don't want anybody else to know about my pen friend, I told you that plainly from the start.'

Then Gordon was possessed by a mischievous

spirit.

'Suppose your pen friend isn't satisfied just with you?' he suggested with a smile. 'Suppose he wants a girl pen friend, too, and that's why the light was shining into Mary's room last night!'

'Don't be daft!' replied Chris, frowning.

'Well, you haven't had any sign of a reply coming yet, have you?' went on Gordon, now annoyed himself.

'Let's go to the rock and see!' said Chris, and they hurried away in the direction of the park. Back on the corner of the road by the school, Mary Francom watched them with interest, and set out to follow them.

She found it hard to keep them in view, for now and again they broke into a trot, but she was sure they were heading for the park. She knew her main problem would be to keep track of them once they had entered it, so she ran fast for the last hundred metres before the park gates. She was rewarded by the sight of them running towards the high mound along a side path, and now knowing their objective, she took her time in order to make sure they didn't see her.

She saw them separate when they reached the path to the rock, Chris climbing upwards and Gordon remaining below, so she hid behind a tree. Soon she became bored with waiting and clearly Gordon was bored too. He scuffed around at the foot of the mound, threw one or two stones up into the horse chestnut trees, and then in desperation threw one up at the rock. The stone fell far short and rolled down to the level ground.

'Hi, Chris!' he shouted. 'Anything happening?'

There was no reply, and Gordon looked at his watch. 'I give you five more minutes,' he shouted. 'I have to go out tonight.'

This brought no answer, and Mary was thinking of wasting no more of her time, when Chris came bounding down the path.

'Any message?' Gordon asked him, loud enough for Mary to hear.

'Nothing,' said Chris. 'I thought there wouldn't be. I haven't had a sign yet.'

'You and your signs!' grumbled Gordon. 'I bet that's the end of it. Come on, I have to hurry.'

They came towards Mary's tree, and when she stepped out from behind it they stopped as if they'd seen a ghost.

'Hullo,' she said sweetly. 'I just happened to be passing. Perhaps you can tell me what you're doing here. It sounds exciting.'

'It isn't,' replied Chris, thinking fast. 'We were only looking for conkers,' he added.

'Do conkers grow on top of the rock?' asked

49

Mary, laughing.

'No, but you can see into the tops of the trees from there - '

'Oh yes - and also receive messages from the conkers telling you where they are! Don't ask me to believe that, Chris. You were expecting a message from somewhere. Don't tell me it was coming by a carrier pigeon!'

'No,' said Chris. 'You must have heard wrongly. Come on, Gordon.'

They left her standing, annoyed and still curious.

'All right - I'll go and have a look for myself!' she shouted. Chris was relieved.

'Good,' he shouted back over his shoulder to her. 'You won't find anything up there.'

By the time Mary had climbed the rock, found nothing there and come down again, the boys were already halfway home.

'We can't possibly tell her,' said Chris as he parted from Gordon. 'If nothing ever happens again, she'll tell everybody, and we'll become a laughing stock. And if anything should happen, I don't want her or anybody else to know about it.'

'I won't tell her anything,' Gordon promised. 'I suppose you'll let me know if you do receive a sign, will you?'

'Of course I will,' said Chris. 'But not if you're

going to laugh about it.'

The sly smile died away on Gordon's face, and he promised to be serious as they went their different ways. Chris was in low spirits as he walked home. He realised how much this strange adventure meant to him, and he dreaded the thought of having to return to an ordinary world in which once again he had no pen friend and a teacher who seemed more and more set on nagging him.

The next day was no exception in this respect.

'Tuck your shirt in, Chris,' Miss Camperdown told him when they returned to the classroom after the dinner hour. 'You look as though you don't care at all about your appearance. You're not an infant any more - you ought to be able to dress yourself.'

'I can, Miss!' Chris tucked his shirt in sulkily, wondering what reason she would find next for picking on him.

He endured the time until the short afternoon break, when he went and sat on a bench at the side of the playground, and spread out some cards of aeroplanes on the bench beside him. Even now he was to be annoyed. Mary ran up alongside him.

'Any signs yet, Chris?' she demanded. 'Going to the park after school again?'

'No!' said Chris, and added rudely: 'Clear off,

will you!'

At that very moment something odd began to happen. The cards on the bench started to flip up and down, some of them rising a few centimetres in the air and landing upside down. Mary laughed.

'That's magic,' she said. Chris felt a breeze

playing around his head, and now the cards were blown down on the playground. He bent down to gather them up before the wind carried them further away. A slight whirring sound accompanied the breeze, but soon both died away. Chris pocketed his cards and ran off to find Gordon.

As they filed back into the classroom the wind was making its presence felt all over the playground, and the teacher on duty hurried the children inside. By the time Chris and Gordon had reached the classroom, there was a howling sound all around the school, and the wind beat against the long picture windows in the classroom. Miss Camperdown, who had a slight headache, secretly grumbled about the wind, and closed all the windows.

A quarter of an hour later, with the wind still roaring around, the Headmaster came into the classroom.

'All the windows closed, Miss Camperdown?' he asked. 'We seem to have a minor hurricane around us, yet if you look at the flag on the church tower it's hardly moving.'

Chris as well as Miss Camperdown could see the church tower in the distance, and there was no doubt that the Headmaster was right - the flag was hanging limply as though there wasn't a breath of moving air near it.

'Very odd,' said Miss Camperdown, who wasn't much interested.

'How are they behaving?' he went on. 'Often high winds make them irritable.'

'Oh, I can't complain,' said Miss Camperdown with a short laugh and a quick look at Chris. She disliked anybody hinting that life in her classroom could be anything less than perfect.

'Oh well, I'll leave you to it,' said the Headmaster, and left thinking that Miss Camperdown sounded a bit irritated herself.

As for Chris, he had forgotten all about the classroom and his work, and was wondering whether the odd behaviour of the cards could be the sign that he was waiting for. He scribbled a little note on a scrap of paper and handed it under the desk to Gordon, to make sure that Mary didn't get to know his thoughts.

'Am going to the park again,' Gordon read. 'I think the wind is a sign for me. Coming too?'

Gordon screwed up the note and nodded agreement. At the end of school time the wind was still blowing hard. It blew them down the path to the school gate, then turned with them and seemed to hustle them in the direction of the park. There was no danger of Mary following, as she was taking part in a netball practice with Miss Camperdown, who was relieved to find that shortly after the practice started the wind had died away altogether.

Chris and Gordon arrived at the rock in record time, and as usual Gordon remained below while Chris climbed to the top. Some children were playing nearby, but the high wind soon discouraged them and the boys were left alone. The wind was swooping this way and that over the rock, and Chris planted his feet firmly on the stony surface in order to keep his balance. As if satisfied that he was there, the wind then retreated, the funnel shape formed above him, and like a leaf blown from the highest branch of a tree, a small shape came swaying from side to side until it landed at his feet.

For a moment Chris stood still, filled with a mixture of wonder, relief and joy. Then he grabbed the letter and came careering down the path from the rock at top speed.

'Another letter, Gordon! Let's go home and decode it!'

He let Gordon briefly inspect the pimpled piece of material, then pushed it into his pocket and began to run. The wind was now the slightest of breezes, and they reached Gordon's home in time to do half-an-hour's work on the new message. As they now knew some of the Morse Code letters off by heart - it's easy to remember that one dot means 'E', two dots mean 'I', three dots stand for 'S' and four dots for 'H' -

they were able to work much more quickly than they had before. By the time Chris had to go home, the translated letter lay before him on the table, and the two of them read and re-read it with fascinated eyes.

'Dear Chris,' it began. 'Many thanks for your answer to my letter. Though we have seen you at long distance, I was pleased to learn more about you and to know how you look. You say that you have two arms and two legs. So have we - but we can run on all four, which we have not seen your people doing. This is perhaps because we live for much of our time underneath the surface of our planet, and often have to travel through low tunnels in which we could not stand on two legs. We are white in colour for the same reason. Sometimes poisonous gases come down on our planet, and then we have to live down below until we have blown them away. We have had to learn much more about our atmosphere than you seem to have done about yours - you don't seem to realise how important it is. We became the Masters of the Winds, and because of this we can now use our knowledge when visiting other worlds like yours. That is why we can use the winds in order to send your letters, and don't need to show ourselves. If we wished, we could suck your air away, or send vast storms of wind which could blow your buildings away.

We have tried once or twice to test our powers in this way.'

'He means hurricanes,' said Gordon.

'But we do not intend to do this,' went on the letter. 'We wish to know more about you and your world, so I can give you an invitation. We can send out small vehicles from our spacecraft *Passim*, and by using the winds could land one at the place at which you have received the letters. You could meet me there, and we could find out more about each other. Send me the time at which you have some Earth hours to spare, and I will meet you then. We arrange our time much better than you, so you will not be with us long enough to cause your adults to worry. If you are afraid, you may bring with you your male friend and the female who is wondering what you are doing. My females would like to meet a female of your kind. Please answer soon.

Yours sincerely,
Peter A.R.'

'Are you going to write back?' asked Gordon.

'Of course I shall write back,' replied Chris, pocketing the letter.

'But - I mean, are we going to do what he asks?'

'It's going to mean telling Mary. If we turn up without her, he might not be pleased, and who

57

knows what he might do then!'

They looked doubtfully at each other. Chris stood up and moved to the door.

'I can't say for sure what I'll do,' he said. 'I'd better be going now. Bring the book to school tomorrow, Gordon. We might need it. I know one thing, though - my pen friend writes back quicker than all the others do!'

As he walked home he was trying to weigh up in a sensible manner the best way of dealing with this new situation. By now he was proud of his unusual pen friend, and a little less worried about telling one or two other people about him. Why should he keep this sensational news to himself? He'd been jealous of all the others when they had pen friends and he didn't have one himself, and now there would be much fun in making them jealous in their turn. He decided to do exactly what Peter had suggested, and tell Mary all about it.

The odd thing was that when he tried to do this, Mary, who had been so curious about what he was doing, didn't wish to waste a moment of her time in listening to him when he approached her in the playground the next day. He came to school early, because he knew that Mary was dropped by her mother outside the school at half past eight in the morning, when she was on the way to work.

'But it's important, Mary - I can tell you now why Gordon and I went to the park. I couldn't tell you before this, because we were sworn to secrecy.'

'Well, now you've left it too late,' declared Mary, continuing to wind her skipping rope around her hand. 'I just can't be bothered any more. If you swore to keep it secret, why don't you go on doing so? Secrets like that aren't worth keeping, or telling.'

'You don't understand,' pleaded Chris, his forehead furrowing up as he frowned. 'We didn't promise one another to keep it secret - we promised someone else.'

'Who?' demanded Mary. 'And what difference does it make?' She started to skip again.

This was so annoying that Chris decided he'd have to give more away before she would change her mind.

'We promised my pen friend,' he said.

'Your pen friend? You've been sulking ever since you found out that you hadn't been given a pen friend.'

'Well, I have one now. A very special pen friend.'

'Ha! Ha! Show me one of his letters!'

'I will do, because in the last there is an invitation to you to come and meet him.'

Mary stopped skipping.

'An invitation to me? Why me?'

'Because he realised that you were trying to find out what was going on. He wants to meet the three of us.'

Mary's curiosity was aroused again, but she wanted quick proof.

'Tell me where he comes from and I'll look at the letter,' she said.

'He comes from a spacecraft,' said Chris, risking everything. 'He sends his letters to me on the rock in the park. He told Gordon and me to keep it a secret.'

'So your friend's an astronaut,' said Mary, laughing.

'No, he isn't. He's a - a sort of boy from another planet. He's circling around in our Universe in a spacecraft called the *Passim*.'

'Look,' said Mary, 'it's not April the first. Stop fooling me, Chris. Go and play football, or marbles - '

'If you saw the letter you'd believe me,' insisted Chris desperately.

'All right - show it to me, then!'

'I can't, here,' explained Chris. 'Other children are coming into the playground, and the secret still has to be kept between the three of us. Come to the far corner of the playground, and I'll show you the letter and the translation we've made from it. Then later on we can talk about it more fully.'

Chris was so serious that Mary decided to humour him. Skipping could be done any day, so it might be more amusing to play his little game and tell all her friends about it afterwards.

'Come on, then!' she agreed, and skipped to the far corner of the playground, where there was a huge log on which they could sit.

'Here's the real letter,' said Chris. 'I bet you've never seen any paper like that before.'

Mary examined the paper and held it up to the

light. 'It's funny stuff,' she admitted. 'But it's full of little dots and lines. There's no message on that.'

'Yes there is. It's the Morse Code, which the people on the spacecraft heard being used and worked out. Gordon and I can read it too. Now look at what we've worked out from it. Read this!'

He sat back and watched with satisfaction as she read the letter and saw the invitation.

'I still think you could have made it up,' she said. 'You could have put those dots and dashes on yourselves.'

'But could I make dots and dashes like that which would disappear when they're put in water?' asked Chris. 'Peter told me to do that, then I can use the same stuff to send my letter back to him, if I want to.'

'Show me that, and I'll believe there's something strange about it,' said Mary.

'And if it does do as I say it will, you'll have to promise to keep it secret,' said Chris. 'But first I'd like you to come to the rock with us when I send off the reply. Here comes Gordon - he'll tell you that all I've said is true. Until we've proved it to you, you won't tell anyone else, will you?'

'I promise that,' agreed Mary, and Chris put the two letters back in his pocket.

After Gordon had confirmed all that Chris had said, and Mary had been reminded of the strange lights she had seen in the sky some nights before, she said she'd think the matter over that evening and give them her answer in the morning.

That night the strange lights returned. Mary, who hadn't been able to sleep because she was puzzling over whether she should join in with the two boys, saw them at half past eleven at night. She stood by the window and watched the swaying disc - and when she left her bed she must have attracted the attention of her parents, who were just coming to bed themselves. They stood by her and studied the lights.

'What a curious effect,' said her mother.

'What do you think it can be?' Mary asked her father.

'I don't know,' he admitted. 'I've never seen anything like it before. In the autumn there is plenty happening in the sky - meteors shooting across it, and of course the Northern Lights causing strange effects. No doubt it can all be explained.'

'But these lights are in the south,' said Mary, who knew her room faced south.

'That's true,' agreed her father. 'You'd better get back into bed now, or you won't be fit for school in the morning.'

Mary obeyed, and at that moment decided she would throw in her lot with Chris and Gordon. Perhaps then, she thought, she would be able to show her father that the strange lights had an explanation more unusual than he thought.

She slept well, and was in the playground as usual at half past eight the next morning. Chris and Gordon arrived early, for them, and sought her out.

'There were more lights in the sky last night,' said Chris. 'My dad saw them.'

'So did mine,' said Mary, 'and he couldn't explain them. I still think you could have made up all this business about the letter - but if I could surprise my dad, well, it's worth taking a chance. When are you going to send off the reply?'

'We've made a rough copy of it,' said Chris. 'If you agree with it, we'll put it in Morse Code today and send it off after school. Can you come then?'

'As long as it's soon after school.'

So much of the free time of the school day was spent in dodging into corners and hiding places in order to complete the reply in secrecy. There was a moment of danger when Miss Camperdown, who was on playground duty, discovered them hidden behind the sports store studying the Morse Code. They weren't doing anything wrong, but Miss Camperdown was not in favour of children being tucked away in corners.

'You'd better be off and run around the playground for a while,' she said. 'You'll catch colds sitting there reading, or whatever you're doing.'

'Yes, Miss,' said Chris, and they hurried away.

'I was afraid she'd want to know exactly what we were doing,' said Gordon.

'Yes, and if she found out she'd probably say it was nonsense and take the letter away,' said Chris. 'She's like that.'

The meeting time was fixed for around five o'clock in three days' time, because Chris had decided that he wanted to allow his pen friend time to make all the necessary arrangements.

'How long does it take for the letter to be delivered?' asked Mary mischievously. 'It doesn't need a first class stamp, does it?'

'We must give them time to make arrangements,' replied Chris seriously.

After school the three of them set off for the park, and when they arrived there they couldn't go up on the rock at once because a mother had taken her toddler up the winding path to look at the rock. They pretended to search for conkers down below, and had found quite a few before the mother and child came down.

'This time,' said Chris, 'you can both come up

65

and watch what happens. You've been invited, and if anything does happen Mary will know that I haven't destroyed the letter myself.'

They followed him up, and stood beside him as he put the paper down on the ground in front of him and waited. Gordon and Mary were silent, as if afraid that if they talked some kind of spell might be broken.

'You don't have to keep quiet,' Chris told them. 'I don't think talking makes any difference. The only thing is, they may not have been following what we are doing.'

He had only just finished speaking when a breeze sprang up, clouds gathered and the funnel between the clouds formed just as Chris had seen it before. The paper on the ground appeared to come alive, bobbing from side to side and then taking to the air, until it disappeared up the funnel.

'It's all true!' whispered Mary.

'I told you so,' said Chris, but curiously, now that she believed him he became scared about what was happening.

'We might as well go down now,' said Gordon, but Chris was not ready.

'The funnel hasn't gone yet,' he said. 'Usually it disappears almost at once. Wait a moment.'

They waited, and still the funnel shape remained.

66

'Look!' called out Mary. 'There's something coming down again!'

She was right. A small piece of paper was coming down towards them.

'It's coming back!' said Gordon, as the paper made its swaying descent.

'No! It's not the same one!' declared Chris, as it landed at his feet. 'It's much smaller.'

He picked it up, and they all studied it.

'There's a very short message on it,' said Gordon. 'I think I can work it out without the book.'

Slowly he read out the letters formed by the dots and dashes: 'Thank you. We will meet tomorrow one hour later your time. Goodbye. Peter.A.R.'

Now they stared at each other, finding it hard to believe what they had heard.

'That's quarter to six,' said Mary. 'Soon after that the park gates close.'

'Don't worry,' said Chris. 'I know a way out.'

'That's not what I'm worried about,' said Mary. 'It's all so quick. I've hardly had time to think about it.'

'Peter must have had the answer ready,' said Chris. 'They must have sent one of their smaller craft out from the *Passim*.'

They looked up into the sky again. While they had been studying the message, the funnel had

67

vanished and the clouds were dispersing. They walked home together, and when they parted and said, 'See you tomorrow,' the words had a special meaning for them which sent them home with serious expressions on their faces, and thinking hard.

4

Betrayed

When Chris opened his eyes the next morning he could think of little else but the meeting arranged in the park, and as time passed so his impatience with everyday life grew. Mary and Gordon were equally restless, and Miss Camperdown had a hard time of it when she tried to hold their attention. The best of teachers can have trouble when children have something special to look forward to in the evening, like a birthday party or a visit to a pantomime, so Miss Camperdown should not really have blamed herself when Gordon and Chris whispered together, nor when Chris shuffled about under his desk to have another look at the message, just to make sure it was real.

But Miss Camperdown thought she was failing, and the thought made her angrier with the children.

'Let me have a look at the message,' whispered Mary to Chris. 'I haven't seen it today. You haven't put it under water yet, have you?'

'Of course not,' whispered back Chris. 'Put your hand out under the desk, and I'll pass it across.'

At that moment Miss Camperdown pounced.

'What have you in your hand, Chris Collings?' she demanded. 'Bring it to me at once!'

Chris stared at Mary and Gordon in desperation, but they couldn't help.

'Nothing, Miss,' said Chris, and dropped the paper on the floor.

'Show me your hands!' demanded Miss Camperdown.

Chris raised his empty hands for inspection, and tried to tell Gordon with a glance downwards that he should rescue the paper. Miss Camperdown was on the warpath, and Gordon didn't react quickly enough. She jumped from her chair and peered underneath the table at which Chris, Gordon and Mary were sitting.

'Mary Francom - pick up that piece of paper and give it to me!'

'It's nothing, Miss - ' said Mary, hesitating.

'Do as I say!'

There was no escape. Mary bent down, picked up the note and handed it to her teacher.

'Get on with your work!' demanded Miss Camperdown, and went back to her chair to look closely at the scrap of paper which was the cause of the trouble. There was, as far as she could see, nothing written on it. She had expected to be able to read some nonsense on it - perhaps even a comment on herself - but this bit of paper was most uninteresting. She gave it a moment's further inspection, and decided that the slightly raised marks on it meant that it could be some kind of wrapping paper. She thought of putting it straight in the waste paper basket, but decided not to because she didn't want to give the children the possible pleasure of taking it out again when she was not in the room. So she dropped it into the drawer in her desk, and found she was even more annoyed that the children should be more interested in a blank piece of paper than in her lesson.

'I'm tired of your silly behaviour,' she told them. 'You can stay in at playtime.'

One of the troubles with Miss Camperdown was that when she was angry she didn't stop to think before she spoke. When playtime came she realised it would be a nuisance to have three children in the classroom when she wanted to put some more lipstick on and have a cup of tea in the staff room. To get round the difficulty she went out of the room, but stayed along the corridor talking to a fellow teacher.

While she was gone the three victims of her anger weren't working.

'How could I be so stupid as to lose the letter!' said Chris.

'It was my fault,' said Mary. 'It's just that I'd been thinking about it since yesterday, and I wanted to make sure it was really there.'

'Don't worry,' said Gordon. 'She'll never find out what it really is.'

'But suppose we need it with us,' pondered Chris.

'As a sort of pass?' suggested Mary. 'I don't think it would make any difference.'

'She put it in her drawer,' said Gordon. 'I'll see if I can get it back.'

'But she'll know!' objected Mary, not wishing to face further punishment. As a favourite net-ball player she was not used to facing Miss Camperdown's anger.

'She won't notice it,' said Gordon. 'We'll hide it somewhere, and even if she is angry, it's more important that we have the letter. It might be important one day.'

With that the sturdy Gordon crept from his place and went to the other side of Miss Camperdown's desk. With a quick look at the door, he pulled at the drawer.

'She's locked it!' he called out to them.

'Quick! She's coming!' Mary warned him.

Miss Camperdown, having finished her chat, had decided that the time was ripe for her to come back and forgive the wrongdoers. She arrived at the door just as Gordon was making for his seat.

'Gordon! What are you doing out of

72

your place?'

Gordon sat down, his face as red as a misty sunset.

'My pen, Miss,' he blurted out. 'It rolled on the floor.'

It was a poor excuse, as the pen was lying on the desk, but fortunately Miss Camperdown was too ready for her cup of tea to hang about asking Gordon questions, so she dismissed them with a warning.

They stayed together in the playground.

'Why did she lock the drawer?' wondered Chris.

'She generally does. She leaves valuables in there sometimes,' said Mary. 'I've seen her do it before we go to netball practice.'

'Do you think she suspects something?' Chris was still uneasy.

'Of course not,' Gordon assured him. 'That kind of person doesn't look for oddities. She has everything planned. She'll throw the paper away when she thinks we're not looking.'

Chris became aware that Stephen Priest, another friend of his, was hovering around near them, and showing interest in their serious discussion.

'Stephen's looking suspicious,' said Chris. 'I think we'd better keep away from each other in the playground for the rest of the day, because we don't want anybody else to follow us to the park this evening.'

'There's not much danger of that,' said Gordon, 'because we'll have to go home first. But we might as well stop Stephen sniffing around now.'

So they broke up the meeting, and kept away from each other at dinner time and during the afternoon playtime. They also managed to behave well enough to keep out of trouble in the classroom until the final bell rang. They arranged to meet at the park gates at half past five, and each went home to kill time and make excuses for going out again.

It was a cloudy evening, and when they gathered at the gates the park was almost deserted. Very little was said as they made their way to the rock. In a way they were afraid lest nothing happened, but they were also uneasy about meeting this stranger from another world. In a few minutes they were standing on top of the rock, gazing up into the clouds.

'There's not much room for anything to land on here,' said Mary.

'Perhaps it won't land,' suggested Chris. 'Peter may come down the funnel of air to me, like the messages have done.'

'It's sixteen minutes to six,' said Gordon, looking at his watch.

'Nothing's happened yet,' said Mary.

'There's a break in the clouds,' said Chris, pointing high above him. 'That's how it began once before. They're controlling the air currents, and pushing the clouds back.'

They watched curiously, and Gordon checked the passing of a minute.

'Time,' he said, and as soon as he had spoken the funnel began to form. The wind rose, and they could hear the leaves on the nearby trees rustling.

'There's nothing in the funnel yet,' said Chris. 'That's odd - the clouds are closing in above the funnel. That doesn't usually happen.'

'I'm scared!' said Mary. 'The wind's trying to pull me off the rock, first one way and then the other - '

'Link arms!' cried Chris, and they held on to one another as the rushing sound of the wind increased to a howling.

Suddenly there was a rush of wind all around them, and it was as though the rock was trying to push them away from it.

'Help!' cried Mary. 'I'm being blown away!'

There was no help for her, nor for Chris and Gordon, as a huge gust of air closed in around them and lifted them high in the air, into the centre of the funnel. They were soon spinning round like tops, and before they could cry out, giddiness overcame them, and it seemed to

them as if the clouds closed in on them. After that, they knew no more. The park-keeper came to the door of his hut, wondering at the strange behaviour of the wind, which had risen so quickly and died away again just when it seemed a storm was about to break. He thought he might have heard a faint cry, and listened for a while, but the park was silent.

'Don't know what's happening to the weather these days!' he mumbled, and set off on his final tour of the park before it was due to close.

Mary, Chris and Gordon remained in a dream-like trance until each felt a hand shaking their shoulders. Chris was the first to awaken, and he saw a dome-shaped roof above him, criss-crossed with what looked like white plastic girders. He sat up, and saw that he was in a huge circular room, off which were a number of doors, about twice the size of doors on Earth. He also saw that the two pillars which were astride of him were in fact the long legs of a tall person who was standing over him. The figure was holding a long rod, and was dressed in a kind of white boiler suit, which fitted him closely.

'Where am I?' asked Chris. He received no answer. He looked around him, and saw that Gordon and Mary also had figures standing over them, and that they were both stirring as though waking from a long sleep. As the creature guarding him was clearly not going to answer him, he sat and watched the reactions of the other two when they came to life again.

They both stretched, sat up and looked around in amazement at the domed roof, and then fearfully at the towering figures of the guards standing over them.

'Where are we?' asked Mary - but the guards gave no reply. She stared around her, and saw Chris to the side of her.

'What's happening, Chris? Where is your pen friend?'

'Not one of these, I hope!' replied Chris, looking up at the bald heads of the guards. 'I didn't expect to be taken to one of his spacecraft.'

'I thought they sent out small spacecraft,' said Gordon, also sitting up. 'This is a huge thing!'

'Perhaps if we stand up, they'll take us to Peter,' suggested Chris, and rather hesitantly they rose to their feet.

The guards took the hint, and pointed to one of the doors around the edge of the huge hall. Chris led the way, followed by his guard, then came Mary, followed by hers, and lastly Gordon and his. Chris stopped at the door, wondering whether to knock, but it opened automatically. After a second's hesitation, he entered. With such giants around him, there was no point in trying to argue. The room he had entered was dark, lit only by a dim, bluish light. Mary and Gordon followed him inside, and the door closed, leaving the guards outside.

'I don't think much of this,' whispered Gordon. 'We've been kidnapped!'

'Maybe Peter didn't want to show himself on the rock,' said Chris hopefully. 'Maybe they told him to put us on a spacecraft for the meeting.'

'Then we should have been told!' protested Mary. 'I wouldn't have come if I'd known this was going to happen.'

'Give them a chance,' said Chris, more to comfort her than because he saw much hope of a quick release ahead.

At this moment another door, this one at the back of the room, opened slowly. Through the doorway came a short, squat figure with a large bald head. It seemed to bring its own light with it, for suddenly the room was bathed in a yellow glow, which shone particularly brightly on the three children. The figure sat at a metallic look-ing desk over which they could only just see his head and neck. He had the same shape of head and leathery skin as the guards, but he was so much smaller that Chris found it hard to believe that he belonged to the same species.

'Welcome to the spacecraft *Passim*,' said the new arrival slowly. 'You are the first creatures from Earth to come here.'

'The *Passim*!' said Chris in surprise. 'That's the main spacecraft. I though Peter was going to visit us in a small craft.'

'We do not wish to risk discovery yet,' replied the figure. 'We do not yet know how hostile your people are.'

'You brought us here without telling us what was going to happen!' protested Chris. 'I was expecting to meet my friend Peter, not to be taken unconscious to your base.'

''We wish to study you more closely,' was the reply - and the three of them exchanged anxious looks.

'Our people are more hostile than you think,' said Gordon boldly. 'If we are missed, there could be trouble for you.'

'Trouble? What trouble?' The little figure's shoulders moved up and down, as if he were laughing.

'Rockets and nuclear weapons,' said Gordon defiantly. 'You might be blown out of the sky.'

'I think not,' came the comfortable reply. 'We are much too far away from Earth.'

This was worrying news, and Chris decided it would be better not to pursue the matter at the moment.

'I was supposed to meet my pen friend, Peter,' he said. 'Why don't you bring him to me?'

'Your pen friend Peter?' The shoulders bobbed

up and down again. 'Yes, I can bring you your pen friend Peter. Wait one moment.'

He pressed a knob on the desk, and out of the wall at the back slid a long, black box.

'Come and look at your pen friend Peter,' said the figure. Chris walked over to the desk, and peered round to see the other side of the box. It was covered with dials and switches, and near the bottom of it was a slit out of which the end of a piece of material protruded.

'That's just a machine,' said Chris.

'That is your pen friend Peter,' said the figure. 'Say "Hullo" to him, and he will answer you.'

'Hullo,' said Chris, feeling foolish. The figure went behind the machine and began to operate a number of buttons. The machine began to buzz, and the material in the slit moved out further. As soon as the buzzing stopped, the figure pulled the material out and handed it to Chris, who saw that it was the same as that used for the other letters from Peter. He waved to Gordon to come to him.

'Look - a message,' he said.

Gordon read the dots and dashes which formed the short message.

'It says: "Hullo, Chris, nice to see you. Peter A.R.," ' said Gordon. The figure, seated again, had wrinkles on its leathery face.

'That's your pen friend,' he said, his shoulders

81

bobbing. 'I am the only person who can speak or understand English on this spacecraft.'

'Betrayed!' cried Chris. 'My pen friend is a wretched machine!'

Angrily he hurled the paper to the floor. The figure at the desk pressed another knob, and the door opened. The guards came in, and the figure waved to them to remove the children. At the same time the light died down and he backed out of the other door, while Chris's so-called pen friend slid back into the wall.

5

No Comfort for Miss Camperdown

The first person to suspect that something was amiss was Gordon's mother. Her husband was already home and the evening meal was waiting - but Gordon had gone out earlier and had not come back.

'He's always back by this time,' she said, and went to the window at the front of the house to see if he was on his way.

'They sometimes forget the time when they're playing,' said Gordon's father, a stout man who had the same steady, calm manner as his son. This was usually a virtue, but now and then, Mrs Welsh would tell her friends, she felt like shaking both of them in order to get some action. This was one of those occasions.

'It's almost dark,' she said. 'He's never out as late as this without telling us, and you know it.'

Mr Welsh shrugged his shoulders and went on reading his paper.

'Well, I'm going to do something, if you aren't!' declared his wife.

'You're not going to ring the police, are you?' he asked. 'I bet Gordon will walk in any moment now.'

'No, I'm not ringing the police. I'm ringing Mrs Collings, Chris's mother. The two of them are usually together.'

Mr Welsh had no objection to this, and his wife made the call. When she had finished it she returned to his side, looking worried.

'Chris isn't in yet either,' she said. 'Suppose something's happened to them, Harold? I shall wish I'd never allowed him out this evening.'

'Oh, nonsense,' replied her husband. 'They're together, and they're not little infants.'

'Nevertheless,' she insisted, 'I don't like it. I wonder if there's anyone else I can ring.'

'There's that boy Stephen Priest,' said Mr Welsh. 'He came to Gordon's party. It's just possible he might know where they are.'

Mrs Welsh was ready to try anybody, so she found Stephen Priest's address in the directory - she knew the road but not the number - and made another call. This time, when she had made it, she stayed by the phone and started dialling again.

'What's going on?' asked Mr Welsh, now showing some ' interest himself, for by now darkness had fallen.

'Stephen says that Chris, Gordon and a girl called Mary Francom have been talking together a lot, and once he saw them together going to the park - hullo, Mrs Francom. Is your Mary at home? I was wondering if by any chance she might know where Gordon and Chris are.'

'I'm so glad you've rung, Mrs Welsh,' said Mary's mother. 'I'm worried stiff about Mary. She hasn't come in either.'

'I suppose if the three of them are together, they may not come to any harm,' said Gordon's mother hopefully - and they agreed to ring again in half an hour.

A half hour is a long time when you are waiting for someone to come in who is overdue, and in all three houses the time dragged on and the families became more and more anxious and uneasy. When the time was up there followed another round of phone calls, this time with the men doing the talking.

As a result of this Mr Collings called the police to report that the children were missing. All police duty cars and constables on the beat were warned to look out for two boys and one girl, and the three fathers themselves toured the streets in their cars in the hope of coming across their children, but all was in vain. At half past ten that night they called off the search and returned to try and comfort their tearful wives. The police, too, cut down the search, believing that there might be more chance of finding the children in daylight.

Promptly at eight thirty in the morning a

police detective turned up at Fairfield School and
awaited the arrival of the Headmaster. They
talked earnestly in his study, and then Miss
Camperdown was sent for. She was preparing for
the first lesson in her classroom, and came un-
easily to the Head's study. There the detective
asked her if she had noticed anything unusual
about the three missing children on the previous

day. She thought hard, but could only report that their behaviour had not been of the best.

'They seemed very restless, and were not able to concentrate on their work,' she said. 'Otherwise I can't recall anything strange.'

After a few more questions the detective let her go, and after she had gone he spoke again to the Headmaster.

'What sort of teacher is Miss Camperdown?' he asked. 'Is she popular with the children?'

'Reasonably so,' replied the Head. 'She takes the netball team, so is liked by the girls in it - and Mary Francom is one of those.'

'She said they were not behaving very well,' went on the detective. 'Is she very strict?'

The Headmaster didn't think so, but perhaps because there was just a shade of doubt in his reply, the detective asked another question.

'To be blunt, could the children have run away because they were afraid of her?'

'I very much doubt it,' replied the Head.

'I'd be obliged if you could question the children further yourself on that side of it,' said the detective. 'They'll take questioning from you much more easily than from a stranger. And ask them also if they saw anything unusual happen in class or in the playground yesterday. You never know - something may occur to somebody.'

The Headmaster waited until half an hour after

the children had started school, then paid a visit to Miss Camperdown's class. The children were working very quietly, as though the three empty seats had made them realise how serious life can be. Miss Camperdown stood up, in the hope that the Headmaster was bringing news of the missing three.

'Stop work, please,' he said. He was so tall and thin that the children in the front had to crick their necks in order to look up at his face. 'I want you all to think very hard about yesterday, and the children who are missing. Did any of you notice anything unusual about them, or did you see which way they went after school? Were they together then, for example, and which way did they go?'

There was silence for a moment or two, then Mary's friend Amy put up her hand.

'Mary went home on her own,' she said. 'I saw her going her usual way.'

'And what about the boys?' asked the Headmaster.

Nobody had seen them going home, but Stephen Priest put up his hand.

'Yes, Stephen?'

'They were talking together in the playground yesterday,' he said. 'They looked ever so serious, as if they were planning something.'

It's easy to be wise after the event, and the

Headmaster thought that maybe Stephen was trying to make things more exciting - or give himself a rest from work by keeping the questioning going a little longer.

'Is that all, Stephen?'

'Yes, Mr Minter. Oh, no! I remember that they were passing a piece of paper under the desk, and it fell on the floor and Miss Camperdown took it away. They were very upset about it, sir.'

'Thank you, Stephen. You can all carry on with your work.' He turned away from the class to talk to Miss Camperdown. 'I suppose there was nothing of interest on that piece of paper, was there?'

'There was nothing on it at all, Mr Minter. As a matter of fact, I think it is still in my desk.' She opened the drawer and brought out the scrap of material, and the Headmaster took a brief look at it.

'Curious, that they should have been bothered about it,' he said. 'There's nothing on it, except some perforations.'

Which shows that you can use very long words and still miss the point. The Headmaster had something else on his mind, and he gave her back the scrap of material, which she put back in the drawer.

'Miss Camperdown, I have to ask you some-

90

thing. Have you been very strict with those three children lately?'

Here was the question which Miss Camperdown had been dreading, the one she had been asking herself ever since she had heard that three of her class were missing.

'Not really,' she answered him. 'I did tell them off for playing about with that piece of paper, and for not getting on with their work, but I think that was perfectly reasonable.'

'Yes - but is it possible that the children took it in the wrong way, more seriously than you meant?'

'I can't believe it,' said Miss Camperdown miserably. 'They've all been told off before.'

'I see,' said the Headmaster, and left her in a turmoil of doubt. Was he going to say that she had been too strict? Had she frightened them? It worried her that she was now thinking of the three children in a different way. Before, they had just been members of the class; now they were very special children, and all she wanted was their safe return. She stood up and went to the window, a tall, willowy figure, wanting to be alone with her doubts and fears.

Amy leaned across to the girl next to her.

'I feel sorry for Miss Camperdown - she looks so upset,' she whispered. There was no comfort for Miss Camperdown for the rest of that long day.

There was no comfort, either, for the police and the parents of the missing three. News of their disappearances was given out on the radio and in the local evening paper, and at five o'clock the police received their first clue. A mother walked into the police station with a toddler, and said she had some information, but she was afraid it could not be much use to them.

'You never know,' said the sergeant on duty politely. 'We're keen to learn about any possible lead, however slight.'

'Well, it was a day or two back - I was showing Gary here the rock in the park. He'd never been up there before, so we went up the path and stood near the top for a while. When we came down I noticed three children scuffling about among the trees at the foot of the mound. They were looking for conkers, I thought, and so I didn't take much notice of them. But when we had gone some distance away I happened to turn round, and I saw them hurrying up the mound to the rock. It was as though they had been waiting for us to go away.'

'Thank you, that could be helpful,' said the sergeant. 'Please tell me the exact time and day, and I'll note it down and pass the information on to those in charge of the case. And I'd like your name and address, please.'

She gave him the details, and he thanked her.

Then, as she turned to the door, she stopped as she recalled something else.

'The funny thing was,' she said, 'that by the time we reached the park gates a high wind had risen, and clouds formed in the sky. It seemed to me that the wind was centred round the rock.'

'Curious,' said the sergeant, but he didn't think it worth making a note of it. Indeed, when she had gone he had a laugh about it with the young constable at the desk.

'The wind started blowing days before they disappeared,' he said. 'How on earth can she expect that to have anything to do with the case!'

'True,' said the constable, 'but they could have been to the park again, and something could have happened there.'

'Now that's another matter,' agreed the sergeant, and picked up the phone.

As a result swift police action was taken, and two police cars paid a visit to the park. Policemen climbed up on the rock, and together with the parents, who had been informed, the small wooded area around the foot of the mound was thoroughly searched. The next day the small duck pond was searched by a diver, who didn't have to do much diving because most of the water only came up to his waist. To the relief of the parents, he brought nothing up but tin cans and some old clothes which had nothing to do

with any of the children.

Asked if he had noticed anything unusual in the park of late, the keeper scratched his head and could think of nothing.

'Oh, there's been some very odd winds around in the past week or so,' he said as an after-thought. 'Once I thought there was going to be a tornado, but it passed away quickly.'

Once again the high winds were, perfectly naturally, ignored, and so the clue of the park, like that of the little piece of material, was dismissed.

'We've drawn an absolute blank,' said one of the detectives to the worried Mr Collings. 'It's as though these three children have disappeared into thin air.'

6

The Spaceship *Passim*

When the bald-headed guards took them away from their unhelpful interview, all three were in despair, but Chris's despair was mixed with helpless anger. Once again his hoped for pen friendship had resulted only in trouble. As the guards strode across the vast area under the glass-like dome, he took in very little of his surroundings. People of varying sizes were criss-crossing the hall, which reminded him of a modern shopping centre - without the shops. There were lifts at various points around the edge of the hall, and some of those walking across it stood still in places coloured a metallic blue, and disappeared downwards. Had he been looking more closely, he would have noticed that the colour of the uniforms of those who went down were also blue, the same shade as the squares on which they had to stand before descending.

Mary saw something else: most of the people in the hall had pieces of what looked like paper in their hands, as if they were carrying messages. The paper, she realised, could be the same material as that of the note which Miss Camperdown had taken from Chris.

For his part, Gordon became aware that the hurrying figures were of very different sizes. The blue ones were all short and stocky; those in black, like some of the guards, were tall and had very long legs and arms. Others, in green, were of medium height, but thin, with rather large heads. Here and there was one dressed in white, who could have been a leader. All were completely bald, and no one spoke as they crossed the hall. Gordon looked hopefully to see if there were any young ones about, but although the blue ones were so short, all of them looked to be adults. The silent, single mindedness of them all Gordon found chilling. Nobody stopped to pass the time of day or even greet anyone. They were, he decided, more like ants than humans.

As they neared the side of the hall, all three of them concentrated on where they were being taken. As they approached some of the doors at the side, they realised that each door had a small square of a certain colour in the middle of it. The guards made for a block of doors with yellow marks on them. One of them opened, and the children were led through the doorway, where they found themselves in a long corridor leading far back - indicating that the spaceship was even larger than they had thought.

One guard walked in front of them, but when

the door closed behind them they realised that the other guards had not followed them. On either side of the corridor were doors, and beside each door was a tiny window. Mary walked directly behind the guard, Gordon followed her and Chris brought up the rear. Daring comes from desperation, and Chris dared to dart to one side to look through one of the little windows. A couple of quick steps and he was back in place again, and found that he could risk this move several times before the guard came to a halt outside one of the doors.

The door opened, the guard indicated that they should enter and when they had done so the door closed again, leaving them alone. They stood in the middle of the little room, looking around them. They were in a cell-like cubicle, with three beds, one over the other, built in the wall on one side, a table firmly fixed to the floor in the middle, but with no chairs, and a small washing area separated by a thin door in the other wall. On the table lay three sets of yellow clothing and three pairs of yellow, sandal-like shoes.

When they had been standing for some time, and nothing happened, they decided they might as well sit down on the bottom bunk.

'I'm sorry about all this,' said Chris. 'It's all my fault. If I hadn't wanted a pen friend, it wouldn't have happened.'

'Not your fault,' said Gordon. 'If Campers had found you a pen friend, you wouldn't have gone to the park, so you could say it was her fault.'

'Oh, what does it matter!' said Mary. 'We're here now - wherever that is - and we'll have to put up with it.'

'I've been cheated,' said Chris. 'They used that machine to trick me. I wish I knew what they want with us here, but what I've just seen makes me afraid.'

'What's that?' asked Gordon.

'I looked through some of the windows as we went along the corridor, and I saw some strange sights. In each one I saw different kinds of creatures - and like in a zoo, each room was made to suit the creatures in it.'

'What sort of creatures?' asked Mary.

'In the first there was a kind of spidery creature, which was hanging from a thick thread which was stretched across the cell. On the floor there were rocks, and some strange, dead insects - food for the creature, I suppose. In the next there was a hairy sort of monkey, but it had horns coming out of its head. It had a tree to climb, and it was eating prickly leaves from it. In the next there was a creature on two legs with short arms and a beaky mouth, halfway between a monkey and a bird. It was eating some meat

which was lying on the floor. The fourth - ugh!'
Chris found it hard to bring himself to describe
it. 'Like a frog with a crocodile's head, I suppose.'

'Nice neighbours we have,' said Gordon.

'Why do you think they're here?' asked Mary.

Chris had an answer, but he was slow to come

out with it.

'I'm afraid,' he said, 'that they are different specimens, brought from the planets which the *Passim* has visited.'

'Then we are specimens,' said Mary.

'Could be,' admitted Chris, and they fell silent again.

After a while Mary stood up and took a closer look at the clothes on the table.

'I may be a specimen, but I'm not going to put that uniform on,' she said. As if in reply, a light shone into the room through an opening which had appeared over the door.

'It is time you put on the clothes provided for you,' came a voice, which could have been that of the figure who had spoken to them before. 'You will put on the clothes, then you will come for some tests, and after that you will be fed and

be allowed to sleep before the next tests.'

'Marvellous,' said Mary, speaking for her own benefit and that of the boys. 'We're human guinea-pigs, aren't we! The only thing is, I'm not going to put this stupid uniform on.'

She sat down on the bed - and received an answer from above the door.

'If you do not dress as desired, there will be no food and no sleep,' said the voice. 'All visitors to the *Passim* must wear the yellow clothes.'

'Even the spiders?' asked Chris - and at once the light went out and a shutter came across the hole above the door.

'They don't seem very friendly,' said Gordon. 'We had better do the tests, and then perhaps they'll let us go home again.'

'I wouldn't be seen dead in that stupid yellow outfit,' declared Mary - and Gordon and Chris kept silent, because they both had the feeling that sooner or later she would have to eat her words.

They sat for a while on the bed, and became aware that the light in the room was fading gradually.

'I'm tired,' said Gordon with a yawn. 'I wouldn't mind lying down.'

Instantly the room was filled with a blinding white light, as though a strong searchlight had been concentrated on it.

'There will be no sleep until the clothes are worn!' said the voice. 'The light will remain as it is until you obey!'

The light did remain at full power, and even when they closed their eyes they were in discomfort.

'We'd better do it,' said Chris at last. 'We don't want to upset them, or we might have no chance of ever returning home.'

At the mention of home, Mary weakened and joined the other two in putting on the yellow uniform, which fitted each one of them tightly but was not uncomfortable to wear. Gradually the white light faded until it was at a normal, bearable level again, then the door opened and a guard appeared. He signed to them to follow him, and they were marched back along the corridor. This time Chris preferred not to look into the windows they passed on their way, but Mary gasped as she saw an ape-like face staring at her through one of them.

They were taken into the central hall under the vast dome, and followed the guard across the middle of it until they came to a square on the floor coloured in yellow, the same shade as their uniforms. The guard pushed them on to the yellow square, then stood back and pressed a round button on the floor with his foot. Slowly they began to descend as the yellow square sank downwards. Soon they were on a level with the guard's huge feet, and then they were in a dark lift shaft.

Mary was seized by a moment of panic.

'Are they going to get rid of us?' she whispered.

'Of course not,' said Chris, trying to sound hopeful. 'We're being taken to the tests.'

The yellow floor of their lift moved below the roof of another corridor, and a fresh guard was ready to receive them when the lift came to a halt. They walked behind him to a yellow door, which opened when he stood in front of it. They were pushed into a huge room, which looked to Chris like a cross between a gymnasium and a science laboratory. The guard had stayed outside, and they were able to look fearfully at some of the odd machines dotted around the floor of the room.

'I don't like that one,' said Mary, eyeing the nearest one to her. 'It looks as though you are supposed to stick your head into that hole.'

Before the boys could think of anything to say, the door opened and the white figure who had first talked to them came in, followed by several others similarly dressed. They were all well under five feet tall and built in the same way, with very large heads and leathery skin. They stood in

104

a line, facing the children and at a respectful distance behind the first figure, who spoke in his one tone voice, as though he were a machine transferring the Morse Code into the English language.

'I am pleased that you have obeyed,' he said. 'It is a great honour for you to be on the *Passim*, which is journeying through space to help bring about something which has never happened anywhere before. You will be helpers in one of the most daring experiments of all time. Tests will be carried out on you, and we must be sure that you can be seen at once by all the members of our crew.'

'What is this experiment?' asked Chris bluntly.

'Time is short,' replied the wrinkled figure. 'Perhaps you will be told later, perhaps not. It is unimportant for you to know.'

'Oh, but it is important to us,' declared Chris. 'If you don't tell me, I don't see why I should do your tests.'

The aged figure was surprised that someone should question him, but decided that at the moment he didn't want any trouble.

'I am not sure that you can understand,' he began. 'We believe we have the oldest and wisest civilisation in the Universe. We have found no other planet containing life as advanced as ours, and we have travelled far. Because of our wisdom, we are able to work out what will happen to our planet thousands of years ahead. In our solar system, our sun has six planets, and we are the furthest away from it. The fifth planet, next to us, is three times bigger than ours, and we have discovered that it is beginning to collapse from inside. We have taken measurements, and it is certain that one day it will disappear, turning into gases which will drift off into space.

'For us, that will mean disaster. The whole balance of our system will be destroyed, and our planet, furthest from our sun, will break away and be torn to pieces. All we have built will be destroyed, all life will come to an end.'

He looked at them so sadly that Mary had to speak.

'I'm sure we're all sorry to hear that,' she said, 'but I can't see how doing tests on us can have any effect on what happens to your planet.'

'Oh, but it can,' insisted the aged figure. 'We have already taken measurements of your planet, and find it to be of almost the same size and weight as the one next to us which is due to collapse. Just the sort of planet we require.'

'But what does that matter - ' began Chris, who was more concerned with his own fate than with that of a planet in another solar system.

'Everything,' replied the figure with an expression of pride and triumph on his face. 'We are thinking of doing what you would call the first planet transplant in the history of time.'

'Planet transplant?' said Gordon. 'I've heard of plant transplants, even of heart and kidney transplants - but planet transplants?'

'Exactly,' said the figure, his wrinkles forming into a shape very near a smile. 'We have the magnetic power to detach your planet from your system and put it into place in ours, as soon as we have broken up the one which is set to collapse.'

They stared at him out of terrified eyes as they tried to grasp the meaning of what he had just said.

'You mean - you're going to take our world and carry it off to somewhere else in space?' asked Gordon.

'Exactly. That is our intention, if all goes well.'

'But the people on Earth - they won't be able to live on a journey through space. And how can you move such a huge object?'

'We shall be taking the air around the Earth as well, and the ozone layer,' he explained. 'The Earth will be kept spinning at its normal rate, and with luck the people on it will hardly notice that they are being transplanted. To you, it seems impossible - to us it is something we must attempt in order to survive.'

'If you say you can do it, why don't you get on with it? Why waste time on us?' asked Chris.

'Because we don't wish to destroy ourselves by bringing into our system a planet which will attack us or poison us. We must make sure the layer of air around your Earth will do us no harm, and that those who live on Earth will be useful to us, if they survive. We are trying out a number of planets during our long voyage, and taking the young from each of them back for inspection, because by the time the chosen planet arrives, only the youngest members on it will still be alive. Now - is there anything more you wish to know?'

The boys stared blankly at him.

'What is your name?' asked Mary.

'Call me Solon,' he replied. 'It means "the wise one". '

'Do the guards who brought us here come from your planet?' asked Chris. 'They are so much bigger than you - they could be a different race.'

'We produce different kinds of people to perform different kinds of work,' answered Solon. 'The guards are the strong ones, and those of us here are the wise ones.' He turned impatiently to the other wise ones. 'Start the tests,' he said, and repeated the order in his own language.

Three of the white robed figures came forward. One beckoned to Chris, another to Mary and the third to Gordon, and the three were led away to different machines. Chris found that his first test involved the giving of a drop of blood from his finger. His escort stood well back, and the machine took the blood in a small tube, which then disappeared inside the machine so that the tests could be carried out. As he moved to the next machine, he heard a sharp cry from Mary, but when he stopped at the sound, his escort pushed him sharply forward.

The second machine was enclosed in a booth, and Chris had to stand on a marked spot while rays of light were directed at him from all levels, either, he thought, to measure him, or to submit him to some kind of X-ray examination. There were machines to test his hearing, the quality of his voice and the rate of his heart beat - and when he came to the sixth machine he realised why Mary had cried out. This machine required that Chris put his head forward into a hole, and then with a tong-like instrument pulled out a tuft of his hair and withdrew it out of sight. Chris yelled too! The final test involved breathing into a container, which then also vanished into the depths of the machine concerned.

One by one they returned to the central point where Solon was waiting.

'One of those things pulled my hair out!'

grumbled Mary.

'I know - it gave me an awful tweak,' agreed Gordon. 'After all those tests, they'll know us inside out.'

'The tests must be performed,' said Solon. 'They will help to tell us more about your planet. You have obeyed, so now you may return and be fed, and then sleep. Tomorrow we shall find out more about you.'

'More!' said Mary. 'There's not much more to know.'

'Yes, there is,' replied Solon seriously. 'We must find out how you move, and how you react to life on the *Passim*. That, too, will help us.'

'When we've done all that, shall we be sent home?' asked Gordon.

'The tests may take a very long time before they are completed,' said Solon, and pressed a button. The door opened, and a guard appeared. The three were led away to the lift and back to their cell.

Mary flopped down on the lowest bunk.

'After all that, I'm hungry,' she said. 'I hope they've had a look at the kinds of food we eat on Earth. I rather fancy some chips, and perhaps a couple of sausages.'

'I wouldn't mind a good cup of tea,' added Gordon. 'If we're going to be here for a long time, that's going to be important.'

'How long, I wonder?' asked Mary.

'They mean to take us back to their planet, along with the spiders and all the other creatures they've collected on their way,' said Gordon.

'I don't see any reason for thinking that,' said Chris, who, because he was responsible for landing the other two in trouble, felt that he should do all he could to keep up their spirits. 'When the tests are done, they won't need us any more.'

Fortunately, further discussion of this unpleasant subject was cut short when the door opened and one of the bald guards brought in a tray which he put on the table and then left, closing the door behind him. They gathered round the tray, on which stood a jug, three bowls and three small boxes.

Chris touched the jug to see if it was hot, then took the lid off it.

'This looks like water,' he said.

'So much for our tea,' said Gordon. 'Let's see what's in the boxes.'

Inside each box were two pills, one white and one yellow.

'So much for my sausages and chips,' said Mary. They stared in disappointment at their so-called meal.

'Might as well try them,' said Chris. 'Maybe they'll taste good.'

Sucking the pills produced no taste at all, and when they drank the liquid it resembled tap water.

'I wonder how often they'll feed us every day,' said Mary. 'I can't say I look forward to my next meal - once a day would be enough of this for me.'

The light began to fade, surely a hint that they should go to sleep, and they took off their yellow uniforms and lay down on their bunks, not to sleep but to think depressing thoughts about their fate and that of the Earth when it was transplanted through space. Now and again they could hear footsteps moving along the corridor outside, and Chris believed that the window at the side of the door must now be open, so that their captors could keep watch on them, just as they did on the other creatures they were holding prisoner.

They became drowsier - perhaps the effect of one of the pills - but still their fears kept them awake. Chris made a final attempt to calm the other two down.

'As soon as the tests are over, I shall ask that we be returned home,' he told them. 'It's clear that they could do it if they wanted to, particularly while the *Passim* is anchored in this part of space. Who knows, we may be quite near to Earth, really.'

'I do hope so,' said Mary, with not much hope in her voice. 'I'm sleepy now. Goodnight.'

In a short time the power of the yellow pills overcame their restlessness, and they dozed into an uneasy sleep. Mary dreamed of sizzling sausages and crisp chips, and Gordon of the Earth hurtling through space to take up its new position. Chris dreamed he was leading an escape from the *Passim*, with Mary and Gordon behind him and all the other strange captives following after them.

One of the guards closed the little window from the outside. They were scheduled to awaken after exactly eight hours of sleep.

7

A Letter for Miss Camperdown

They were awakened eight hours later when the light gradually intensified until they were afraid it might become unbearable as once before, and sprang out of their bunks. At once the light decreased to a normal level. They put on their yellow clothes, and soon afterwards the guard appeared with another jug of water, but no pills.

'Are we supposed to live on a couple of pills a day?' complained Mary.

'Looks like it,' said Gordon. 'I can't say I'm feeling very hungry yet.'

'Nor me,' agreed Chris, who had other matters than food on his mind. He was not convinced that they would be set free after the tests, and he had been trying desperately hard to think of a way to convince Solon that it would be best to allow them to return to Earth. There was no certain way, but he resolved to try any slim chance which presented itself. Timing was important - whether he should try and speak to Solon before the second group of tests began, or whether he should wait until they had been completed. He decided to wait - after all, there was just a chance that Solon would tell them at the end of the tests that they could go.

The guard appeared, and they were marched off in the same way as on the previous day - along the corridor, across the central hall, down the lift and into the testing area.

If anything, Solon was looking more serious than ever.

'Most of the results of your tests have been given to me,' he said. 'We find it is worth going on with the next set, which are aimed to reveal how you are constructed. Follow me.'

They followed him through a doorway at the end of the room, which led them into what at first seemed to be an open air exercise area. But way up above them stretched a transparent roof, looking out into the blankness of space.

Here the three were put through their paces. They had to demonstrate how they ran, how they jumped, how they bent their arms and turned their heads - and all the time small, white uniformed people, members of the wise section on *Passim*, entered notes on machines. Finally, they had to stand in front of a machine which sent out rays which clung around their bodies, perhaps recording their shape or even charting the whole make-up of their bodies.

After all this they were as exhausted as if they had been playing a hard game of football or netball.

'You have done well,' said Solon. 'No more will be required of you until you have been fed and rested.'

Chris decided that the moment had come to speak.

'When the tests are ended, will you be sending us home?' he asked.

'Home?' said Solon. 'This is your home. We shall need you as proof to convince our rulers that all we tell them about Earth is true.'

The three stood silent and motionless as they took in the meaning of what he had said. So did men receive the news of the death penalty in the old days, when the judge put on the black cap.

The silence was broken by a loud buzzing sound which appeared to come from Solon's chest. He pulled a flap in his uniform aside, and revealed a small black box attached to his chest. He flicked a switch, and a jumble of sounds could be heard - maybe coming from a voice or from a machine.

Wherever it came from, the effect upon Solon was startling. He stepped several paces back from the children, flipped off the switch and called for the guard. When he approached, Solon waved the children away, and the guard hurried them back to the central hall. As they passed through, they noticed that the figures criss-crossing the hall kept well away from them, and some of them directed curious glances at them as they passed.

Soon they were shut in their cell - and the little window was closed, as if the guards were no longer required to keep a check on them.

'Well, that's it!' said Mary, flopping down on the bed. 'We'll never see home again.'

Tears were in her eyes, and the other two brushed their arms across their faces once or twice so as not to show their own feelings.

'And all because I didn't have a pen friend,' said Chris bitterly. 'As if that mattered one penny!'

'It's Miss Camperdown's fault,' said Gordon, trying to comfort him. 'She should have realised that you cared.'

'At least they could let us send a letter home,' said Mary, sobbing quietly.

'Nobody would find it, I suppose,' said Gordon. 'Anyway, I don't think they'll want to make any more contact with Earth - unless they let us join up with it when it's transplanted! We'll be as old as the hills by then,' he added glumly.

Chris said nothing, but Mary's mention of sending a letter started him thinking.

'We must try to find an excuse for them to let us send a letter,' he said after a while - but hard as he thought, no excuse occurred to him.

The silence was broken when the door was

pushed open and a trolley with a jug and three boxes was pushed just inside it. The door closed again, and the guard had not shown himself at all.

'They're becoming less friendly,' said Gordon.

'I wonder why,' pondered Chris. 'Solon wanted to be rid of us as soon as he received that message.'

'Maybe there's a rocket coming up from Earth - '

Mary started to cry again at the thought of how unlikely her idea was, and so Gordon didn't finish his sentence.

'If they did, it wouldn't do us much good,' said Chris. 'We'd better take these pills and have a drink - it's no good giving up altogether.'

They were still drinking the water when the little window was pushed open.

'Please listen!' said a voice from the corridor.

'It's Solon,' whispered Gordon. 'What can have brought him to our corridor? I thought he was too important to come.'

'Listen,' repeated Solon. 'I have to tell you that the position is completely changed. You will not have to do any more tests.'

'Hurrah!' said Mary.

'The reason is,' went on Solon, 'that we have found out through one of our first tests that we cannot allow you to remain for very long on board the *Passim*.'

'Hurrah!' said Mary again - but Chris was more cautious, and urged her to be quiet. There was a pause, and when he went on Solon's voice showed irritation.

'The news is not so good for you. When we tested your breathing, we discovered that when you breathe out our air, you fill our atmosphere with a poison which slowly affects the air around it. As we shall be travelling on the *Passim* for a long time to come, in the end your breath would pollute all our air. The air we breathe out ourselves can be put through our air cleansing machines which purify our atmosphere, but yours could not be cleansed, but would go on poisoning us. So we are no longer interested in your Earth, because your air mixture would in the end kill us off. I am also sorry to say that we cannot keep you much longer on the *Passim*.'

'What are you going to do with us?' asked Mary.

'You will feel no pain,' said Solon, as if he were being very kind. 'You will be given something to send you to sleep, and then you will be set free.'

'Set free!' cried Gordon. 'You mean we shall be put out of the *Passim* and left to float about in space for ever! You can't do that to us! Chris, they're worse than the pirates who used to make their enemies walk the plank! If I could smash

121

up this rotten spaceship before I went, I'd do it.'

'Just a moment,' said Chris. 'Why can't you send us back to Earth?'

'We haven't the time,' said Solon. 'Now that we know that your Earth is not right for us, we cannot afford to delay. And you might tell your people about us, and we want to travel through space without attracting any attention. We cannot allow any attempt to challenge our superiority.'

'How many Earth days have we been here now?' asked Chris, while Mary and Gordon looked at him, puzzled.

'It will soon be the night of the third day,' replied Solon. 'Why do you ask?'

'Because by now there will be a big search on for us,' said Chris, 'and since my teacher took away a letter you sent to me, they will find out that we have been taken from the rock, and they will connect up the strange lights and the high winds they have seen, and they will know that we are somewhere out in space. That is to say, the secret experts on space will know that. How far above the man-made satellites are we?'

'We can see them easily,' said Solon.

'Then we are still within reach of up-to-date rockets,' went on Chris. 'They'll be able to detect the presence of *Passim* in the sky, and who knows what they will do then! Your spaceship may never reach the home planet, and all your work will be wasted.'

Solon was silent for a moment, for Chris's long speech had given him much food for thought.

'You were told to put all the letters in water,' he said. 'Why did you disobey?'

'I didn't disobey,' said Chris firmly. 'Miss Camperdown took it away from us, and put it in her desk. She's bound to think about it and give it to the police, and then the truth will come out. There's only one way to avoid this, and that is to send Miss Camperdown a letter at once, and tell her to bring the letter to the park. She'll give it up if she thinks that in return we shall be brought back safely.'

'I will think about it,' said Solon, and closed the window.

Chris collapsed on the bed, and the other two stood over him.

'Finish this drink, Chris,' said Gordon. 'It was a very good try, even if he doesn't take any notice.'

'There wasn't much in that last letter,' said Mary.

'Maybe there wasn't,' agreed Chris. 'But they don't know how much can be worked out from the material, and also they don't know the distance to which rockets and satellites can be sent. They just might prefer to send us back and hope no more will come of it.'

'That could depend on one other thing,' said Gordon gravely. 'If they think they can make us forget all about what's happened to us, they might be happier to be rid of us.'

They stretched out on their bunks, very low in spirits at the thought that it would be so much easier for Solon to order them to be thrown out into space. They couldn't sleep in spite of the pills, and when the window was opened again they sprang up together and stood by the table.

'We have decided,' came Solon's voice. 'A letter will be sent first to your teacher, who will then bring that letter and the one she took away from you to the rock at ten hours in the night, when you will be released in exchange for the letters. Here is material. You may write the letter yourself.'

A piece of the familiar material was tossed into the room.

'I haven't a pen - ' said Chris.

'I have,' Gordon called out. 'Hurry up and write it, Chris.'

The fear which comes when there is a chance, but the chance might easily lead to failure, is as hard to bear as the dull fear when there is no hope at all. Beads of sweat stood on Chris's forehead as he struggled to compose the letter to Miss Camperdown. After much thought and some help from the others, he ended up with the following:

'Dear Miss Camperdown,
I am writing to say that we are all safe, and are hoping to come back at ten o'clock on the night after you receive this letter. We can only come if you will bring this letter and the piece of material you took away from me, to the rock on the mount in the park at ten o'clock at night. You must be alone, and you must not tell anyone else about this letter, or we shall not appear. Please be there - it is our only chance.
Signed, Chris, Gordon, Mary.'

Chris made them each sign, then handed it to Solon.

'Read it aloud to me,' commanded Solon, and Chris realised that although Solon had learned to understand spoken English, and to speak it - he couldn't read it. Chris read it out very slowly.

'That will do,' said Solon. 'But where should it be placed so that your teacher can find it?'

'The best place is in the school playground,' Chris told him. 'When the children arrive in the morning, one of them is sure to find it and take it to Miss Camperdown. But it should be put in an envelope with her name on it, or it won't be

kept secret.'

'Correct,' said Solon. 'An envelope? What is that?'

'Bring me some more material, something to cut it with, and something which will stick it together, and I'll make one,' said Gordon. It took some time to arrange for the correct items to be brought, as envelopes were unknown to the members of *Passim*. However, at last material was brought, and a small cutting machine, and a guard was sent in to instruct Chris on how to use it. It seemed that Solon was unwilling to come into close contact with the children himself any more.

At last the envelope was completed, by stitching rather than sticking. Chris inserted the letter and wrote: 'To Miss Camperdown - URGENT!' on the envelope. He handed it to the guard, who stitched the flap down. The guard then handed it to Solon, who was still outside.

'You can now sleep,' Solon ordered them. 'You will be awakened when your craft is ready to go.'

'Will you be coming with us?' asked Mary.

'No one will be coming with you. You will be in a controlled craft, directed from here. We cannot risk a member of the *Passim* being seen by any of your people, and the craft will be programmed to self-destruct if anything goes wrong. You had better have some rest now. Goodbye.'

Solon closed the window.

'Programmed to self-destruct? What does that mean?' asked Mary, who had a good idea of its

127

meaning, but didn't like to face the truth.

'It means they'll blow it up, and us with it, if they think it necessary,' said Gordon.

There was nothing else to do but lie down on their bunks, and it must have been the effect of the pills which allowed them to doze into an uneasy sleep.

When they were awakened, it was to receive another set of pills, which they had to swallow while the guard stood by them. These pills were large and black, and they were surprised when they could walk out of their cell when the guard ordered them to do so, and feel none the worse for swallowing them.

8

The Passing of the *Passim*

Before Miss Camperdown set off for school in the morning she pulled back a lace curtain to see if there were any reporters about. There were none to be seen, but nevertheless when she went out of her front door she made a dash for her car and nervously locked herself inside it in case there was somebody hiding behind a fence.

She had not slept well that night. As the teacher of the class from which three children were missing, she had been interviewed by reporters from several papers, and worse than that, had come to realise that some people thought that she could be to blame for the disappearance of the children.

People were asking whether she had been so strict with them that they had run away. At times she was very angry about this, and at other times she looked back to her lessons with the class and wondered if perhaps she could indeed be blamed. She remembered that Chris had been missed out when all the pen friends had been arranged - but that, she consoled herself, didn't explain why the other two had gone missing.

'It's nonsense!' she said to herself once or

twice, aloud. Miss Camperdown had never talked to herself before, which showed how worried she was. She remembered how before all this happened she would say to children: 'I'm really worried about your work - you'll have to try much harder,' or 'I'm worried about your handwriting - you'll have to stay behind and practise after school if it doesn't improve!'

Worry! She hadn't known what worry was, until these three had vanished. Now, she thought, I have a little idea of what it's like to have children of one's own.

She nearly knocked down a bollard in the school car park as she parked her car, because she was so busy with her own thoughts. If only, when she reached the playground, she could see those children playing there! Life would begin again for her.

But as the playground came in view, only one or two of the children were to be seen, and none of those was Mary, Chris or Gordon. Miss Camperdown had arrived early in the hope of avoiding having to talk to anxious parents or even members of the press wanting the latest news. As she entered the main door of the school, one of the children she had seen in the playground came running towards her.

'Miss Camperdown! Miss Camperdown! I've found this letter for you!'

'A letter? Oh, thank you, Gillian.' Miss Camperdown took the envelope from her, at first thinking it could be from a parent of a child in her class. The material of the envelope was unusual, and yet in a way familiar to her.

'I found it blowing about on the playground, Miss Camperdown,' explained Gillian, an earnest eight-year-old.

'Thank you, Gillian. Well done.'

Gillian ran away, for she saw that the teacher was no longer interested in her. Miss Camperdown was studying the envelope closely. The writing on it looked to be that of a child. She hurried up the stairs and along the corridor into her room, dropped her bag with all the books in it on the floor, and tore open the envelope.

When she read the letter from Chris she had to sit down at her desk, or she might have fainted away. She read the letter several times; then she closed her eyes to think, opened them and read it again. Her first thought was to rush off and share the news in it with anyone who might have arrived at school - best of all, the Headmaster. Only the warning in the letter stopped her - she couldn't risk doing anything to prevent the three children coming to meet her.

Next, she wondered if the letter could be a cruel joke played on her by some twisted adult, or even a child. She studied the handwriting, then hurried to Chris's desk and took out his books. She found his English book, and compared the handwriting in it with that of the letter. No doubt at all, the writing was Chris's! Then she remembered the piece of paper she had taken from him, and went back to the drawer of her desk to find it. For a few frantic seconds she couldn't see it, and wondered if she had absent-mindedly thrown it away. She felt in the back of the drawer - and there it was! She pulled it out and compared the material with that of the letter. It was exactly the same.

Puzzled, she put them both in her handbag. Where could those children have gone, to find someone with such odd writing paper? The answer would have to wait until ten o'clock that night, and now her problem was to last out the day without giving away her secret. She kept away from the other teachers as much as possible, and kept the class busy with work from books, because she couldn't concentrate on teaching them, her mind was so fixed on what would happen that night. Further, less pleasant ideas occurred to her. Could the letter be a trap, so that she would be attacked and kidnapped when she went to the park? For the sake of finding the lost children, she would have to risk all this, she decided - but she would take with her a sharp knife, some pepper to throw in the face of an attacker, and a whistle to blow in the slight hope of raising the alarm should all go wrong.

At playtime she had to go down to the staff room, for her absence would have been unusual. She sat in a corner and pretended to read a magazine on how to teach children to make puppets, but only managed to spill some tea over it. Luckily, the other teachers were busy talking about what one or two of them had seen during the night.

'At two o'clock in the morning I couldn't sleep, and when I looked out of the window there were strange lights flickering in the sky,' said Mrs Cremond. 'It really was weird.'

'I was up at about the same time, because Imogen couldn't sleep,' said Mrs Wade.'I saw the lights, and when I looked across in the direction of the school, I saw the trees swaying in the wind. I couldn't go back to sleep for a long while.'

'You'd better tell the local UFO Spotters Society,' said Mr Wilton, laughing. 'They've had lots of reports of flickering lights and high winds lately. Are you sure you didn't see a spacecraft landing?'

'It's not funny!' declared Mrs Cremond. 'You're lucky, if you slept through it all.'

'Probably just a distant thunderstorm,' insisted Mr Wilton. 'These UFO people have good imaginations. Did you see anything, Phyllis?'

Miss Camperdown sat up straight, then shook her head.

'No - but I did hear the wind blowing very hard at one time,' she replied, and took her teacup to the sink and left. On the way to her classroom the moment she had dreaded and hoped to avoid happened. The Headmaster opened his door just as she was passing.

'Not a sign of those children yet,' he said. 'I think the police are beginning to fear the worst. No clues from the rest of the class, I suppose?'

'I'm afraid not,' said Miss Camperdown, and hurried away in fear of being tempted to give away her news.

She must have looked guilty as she made for the stairs, for he went into his office and spoke to his secretary about it.

'Poor Miss Camperdown - I think the whole thing is getting her down,' he said. 'She looks very upset about it all.'

'So would I be, if three of my class were missing,' said the secretary, in a tone of voice which could have meant that she thought Miss Camperdown was to blame.

The Headmaster quickly returned to his own room, and sat down to wonder about the same thing.

The school day dragged on for Miss Camperdown, and back in her own flat afterwards the minutes passed even more slowly. She pecked at a small meal, drank plenty of hot tea and swallowed a calming pill, then arranged her knife, torch and whistle in the pockets of a leather jacket and waited for her time to come.

At half past nine she set off for the park, and

arrived there at quarter to ten. The big iron gates were closed, and she was not equal to climbing over them, but she had planned for this. She made her way along the outer fence until it came to an end and a hedge took over the task of keeping people out. Children, she knew, were not put off by this barrier, and sure enough she came across a gap low down near the ground. Making sure no one was about, she first went down on her knees, then found the only way to squirm through the gap was by lying flat on the ground.

To her relief nobody spotted her while she was engaged in this odd behaviour, and once through the hedge she made her way to the path which led to the mound and the rock. It was a dark, cloudy night, and as she climbed the path up the mount she had to switch on her torch in order to check the time. She was standing on top of the rock at five minutes to ten, a lonely figure looking out into the darkness above and beyond her. Slightly below her the lights of a part of Fairfield twinkled.

'I'll stay until quarter past ten,' she vowed. 'If nothing's happened by then, it must have been a hoax.' She placed the papers on the ground in front of her and waited.

At three minutes to ten the branches of the trees began to sway, and by two minutes to ten strong gusts of wind were blowing around her, and a star was visible in a small patch of sky above her. At one minute to ten strange lights were hovering over the rock, and the lights moved from side to side. Miss Camperdown became frightened and giddy - and at ten o'clock the dizziness overcame her, and she collapsed on the ground in a faint.

She was only unconscious for a few seconds, and when she opened her eyes the wind had died down, the clouds covered the sky again - and three children were standing over her.

'Miss Camperdown - are you all right?' asked Chris.

'We're back, Miss Camperdown!' said Mary.

She struggled to her feet, clasped all three in her arms, and was so happy that she nearly fainted again.

'This is wonderful!' she said. 'I shall take you all home, and tell the Headmaster, and the police - everyone will be so happy.'

'So are we, Miss,' said Gordon.

Miss Camperdown turned to go, then her mind began to work. She looked down at her feet.

'The letters are gone!' she said.

'What letters?' asked Chris.

'Why, the letters you asked me to bring to the rock,' said Miss Camperdown. 'You must know what I mean.'

For a moment she almost became a strict schoolmistress again.

'But we don't know what you mean,' said Gordon.

'Does it matter, Miss?' asked Mary. 'Can't we go home now?'

'Where have you all been?' asked Miss Camperdown.

All three looked blank, but Chris saw that she expected an answer.

'Can't remember much after we left school, Miss,' he said. 'We came to the park, I think, and it was very windy - and after that I can't remember anything until we came back here.'

'But how did you come back?' asked the puzzled teacher.

'I don't really know, Miss,' said Gordon. 'It was very windy again - and then suddenly we were here.'

'I don't know any more than that either,' said Mary, and all three of them looked so thankful and innocent that Miss Camperdown decided she had better stop the questioning and hurry them home before they disappeared again.

They went to Mary's home first. Her parents were overjoyed, and then started to ask questions.

'Please,' Miss Camperdown begged them, 'call the police and tell them the children are back,

and ring the Headmaster too. We can ask them questions about where they've been in the morning. Now I must take the other two home.'

From being a suspected person, Miss Camperdown became a kind of heroine when she turned up at the homes of Chris and Gordon.

'I don't expect them at school tomorrow,' she said. 'They'd better have a rest.'

She went home and slept properly herself for the first time since they had disappeared. The police visited them all on the next day, but they couldn't find out any more than Miss Camperdown had about where the three had been, so they had to go to a hospital for tests. These tests were much easier and pleasanter than the ones they had endured on the spacecraft *Passim*, but the results didn't reveal anything unusual, as an official told their parents.

'They don't appear to have been harmed,' he explained, 'and they are in good spirits, so it may be best to forget all about the affair. There does seem to be a possibility that they have been given a drug which has affected their memories, but it's hard to know for sure. I should take them away and let them start their normal lives again.'

So the pills had done their work, and the spacecraft *Passim* and Solon and the guards were completely forgotten. Only once did Chris say something which made him feel uneasy, and then no one took much notice of it. Miss Camperdown had welcomed them back to class, and was in an excellent mood.

'I have some good news for you, Chris,' she said. 'Monsieur Legrand has written to me and given me the name and address of a new boy who has arrived at his school, and would like to be your pen friend. I've written the details down here, and you can write to him as soon as you like.'

'I hope he turns out to be real, not like my last pen friend,' said Chris as he took the piece of paper.

'Your last one?' asked Miss Camperdown. 'But all the fuss was because you didn't have one, Chris. What are you talking about?'

'I don't really know, Miss. Thank you, Miss,' said Chris, looking as puzzled as she was.

Maybe it was a sign that the pills Solon had given them won't work for ever, and one day Chris will remember his machine pen friend from another planet. Then, of course, it will be too late for them to make anyone else believe their story, so Solon and the *Passim* will pass away for ever from the Earth. Another mystery is that Miss Camperdown can't explain why she went to the park at ten o'clock that night. 'It must have been instinct,' she says, and everybody is happy to leave it at that.

So much is happening down here on Earth - with pen friends to write to and reports that Miss Camperdown is leaving to marry Monsieur Legrand, which is why she's become such a kind and popular teacher, that the *Passim* will probably have passed unnoticed.

But who knows when some other spacecraft may be nearing our world, and ready to communicate with us? Maybe one day we'll all be able to have pen friends from another planet - unless, of course, we're all transplanted to another solar system, and there won't be much point in writing letters on the journey.